Tammy closed the door and leaned back against it, staying out of the firing line of the volatile aggression pouring from Fletcher as he stalked around, checking out her living space, even poking his head into her bedroom and bathroom

"This place is a shoebox, Tamalyn," he shot at her.

Her chin rose defensively. "I've managed here quite happily for the past seven years."

"It meets a single person's needs. It will not do for you and the baby," he stated emphatically, his gaze dropping to her stomach again.

He scooped up her door key, and the handbag she had laid on the kitchenette counter when she'd grabbed for the telephone.

"Let's move," he said with an air of unassailable decision, striding back to her and gathering her to his side as he reopened the door.

"Where are you taking me?" she asked, alarm at being swept out of the security of her own home kicking her heart out of its numb state.

"I'm taking you to what will be *our* place."

Dear Reader,

Harlequin Presents® is all about passion, power and seduction—along with oodles of wealth and abundant glamour. This is the series of the rich and the superrich. Private jets, luxury cars and international settings that range from the wildly exotic to the bright lights of the big city! We want to whisk you away to the far corners of the globe and allow you to escape to and indulge in a unique world of unforgettable men and passionate romances. There is only one Harlequin Presents®. And we promise you the world….

As if this weren't enough, there's more! More of what you love every month. Two weeks after the Presents® titles hit the shelves, four Presents® EXTRA titles go on sale! Presents® EXTRA is selected especially for you—your favorite authors and much-loved themes have been handpicked to create exclusive collections for your reading pleasure. Now there are more excuses to indulge! Each month, there's a new collection to treasure—you won't want to miss out.

Harlequin Presents®—still the original and the best!

Best wishes,

The Editors

Emma Darcy

RUTHLESS BILLIONAIRE, FORBIDDEN BABY

HARLEQUIN®

TORONTO • NEW YORK • LONDON
AMSTERDAM • PARIS • SYDNEY • HAMBURG
STOCKHOLM • ATHENS • TOKYO • MILAN • MADRID
PRAGUE • WARSAW • BUDAPEST • AUCKLAND

Recycling programs
for this product may
not exist in your area.

ISBN-13: 978-0-373-23608-4

RUTHLESS BILLIONAIRE, FORBIDDEN BABY

First North American Publication 2009.

All about the author...
Emma Darcy

EMMA DARCY was born in Australia, and currently lives on a beautiful country property in New South Wales, she has moved from country to city to towns and back to country, sporadically indulging her love of tropical islands with numerous vacations.

Her ambition to be an actress was partly satisfied when she played in amateur theater productions, but ultimately fulfilled when she became a writer. Initially a teacher of French and English, she changed her career to computer programming before marriage and motherhood settled her into community life. Her creative urges were channeled into oil painting, pottery, and designing and overseeing the construction and decorating of two homes, all in the midst of keeping up with three lively sons and the very busy social life of her businessman husband.

A voracious reader, the step to writing her own books seemed a natural progression to Emma, and the challenge of creating wonderful stories was soon highly addictive. With her strong interest in people and relationships, Emma found the world of romance fiction a happy one.

Currently she has broadened her horizons and begun to write mainstream women's fiction. Other new directions include her most recent adventures of blissfully breezing around the Gulf of Mexico from Florida to Louisiana in a red convertible, and risking the perils of the tortuous road along the magnificent Amalfi Coast in Italy.

Her conviction that we must make all we can out of the life we are given keeps her striving to know more, be more and give more, and this is reflected in all her books.

CHAPTER ONE

The First Wedding

'I'M SORRY you're going to be loaded with Fletch as your partner, Tammy, but we had to make him a groomsman. He *is* my brother and it was safer to include him in the wedding party than try seating him anywhere else at the reception. Being such an arrogant pig he's bound to offend whatever guests shared his table. Stuck at the end of ours, he shouldn't upset anyone, and since you'll be at the other end, you won't have to put up with much of him for long.'

Celine's apologetic, semi-pleading speech was doing a re-run through Tammy Haynes's mind as the limousine carrying the five bridesmaids set off for the church. Although they'd all been friends with Celine since the beginning of high school, none of them had ever met Fletcher Stanton. He'd always been referred to as 'my brother, the brain,' doing 'his thing' overseas, and largely absent from his younger sister's life.

Having flown home to Sydney only yesterday, he'd begged off the wedding rehearsal, pleading jet lag, making Celine gnash her teeth over his lack of caring for her wish for everything to go perfectly on her big day. 'No consideration. Thinks he can just waltz through anything and get it right,' had been her vexed mutter. 'He could have come a day earlier, but I bet he thought it was beneath his intelligence to rehearse anything.'

His formidable intelligence clearly did not win any brownie points from his sister, though it did have to make him a stand-out kind of guy, Tammy thought, her curiosity piqued despite Celine's criticisms of her brother. There weren't too many people in the world who'd achieved what Fletcher Stanton had.

Quite recently there'd been an article about him in *Time Magazine,* headlined Technological Wizard of the Year, detailing how remarkable he was. From an early age he'd been a superstar of mathematics, winning international competitions even before his teens, doing university maths when other boys his age were still finishing primary school, graduating from Sydney University with an honours science degree at sixteen, then being invited to do a Ph.D at Princeton in the USA, which he'd gained at the amazing age of twenty-one.

He'd walked straight out of academic life and

become the driving force behind creating a highly advanced computer system that could track any form of transport anywhere in the world, and he and his team of colleagues were currently making billions of dollars out of it, selling it to governments and Internet companies. None of which changed Celine's sour view of her brother.

'He's even more arrogant since he's made all that obscene wealth,' she had commented in her warning speech to Tammy. 'Everyone kowtowing to him and a heap of gold-digging women feeding his ego to get what he can give them. Don't let him turn your head with his billions, Tammy. Believe me, you wouldn't want to live with him.'

The warning wasn't needed. No way was Tammy going to get hooked into the life of a rich man. She'd seen her mother go down that track all her life, trading on her beauty to snag wealthy husbands who'd ditched her when the desire she'd stirred was replaced by desire for someone else who looked more attractive to them. There'd been no real love in any of those marriages, nor in the affairs that had failed to make it to a wedding. It sickened Tammy to see her mother growing more and more anxious about her looks, becoming a gym junkie to keep slim and fit and resorting to cosmetic surgery to maintain a youthful desirability, as though she wasn't worth anything if she didn't have that.

Being a rich man's brief possession was certainly not on Tammy's life agenda. If she ever did marry, it would be because she truly loved the man and he truly loved her back. Like Celine and Andrew. She decided to view Fletcher Stanton simply as a curiosity, letting any arrogance from him flow right past her, refusing to let anything spoil this special day—the first wedding of one of the gang of six from school.

They'd shared so much together, counting on each other to be there at times of stress, making the joy of any great occasions so much more fun. For Tammy, the bond of their friendship had made up for the emptiness of her home life, giving her teen years a sparkle and warmth that dispelled much of the loneliness of having no family, apart from a mother who preferred her daughter not to be hanging around her neck. Even though the six of them had taken different paths into their twenties, the friendship was still as strong as ever, and Tammy hoped it always would be.

Celine, of course, was in the following limousine with her parents, but the rest of them were here— Kirsty, Hannah, Lucy, Jennifer and herself, thrilled to be fulfilling the pact they'd made years ago, standing shoulder to shoulder as bridesmaids whenever one of them became a bride.

The girls were chatting excitedly and Tammy

joined in the animated conversation, putting the problematic groomsman out of her mind. Hannah was thrilled with the copper streaks in her brown hair, done especially to match up with Lucy's naturally auburn colour. Lined up at the altar there would be two blondes—Celine and Kirsty—two redheads, then two brunettes—Jennifer's hair being dark brown and Tammy's almost black. The dresses were lovely; soft, floaty organza with frills around the neckline and hem. Kirsty was in pink, Hannah in lemon, Lucy green, Jennifer blue, and Tammy mauve, all of which definitely created a romantic, rainbow bridal party.

Delighted with everything, they piled out of the limousine at the church, grinned at Celine as she emerged from her car, joked with her father who was beaming with pride in his daughter, ensured that their bride looked absolutely perfect: veil falling properly, bouquet held just right. Once in the foyer, they checked each other over before lining up for the procession down the aisle, determined on doing their friend proud on this, her day of days.

Tammy felt a flutter of nerves when the music started. She was leading off and was suddenly frightened of stepping out of beat.

'Go!' Jennifer hissed from behind her.

Everyone in the church had turned to look. She made her feet move, concentrating fiercely on how it had been done in rehearsal. Smile, she told herself, seeing the grin on Andrew's face at the other end of the aisle—a happy man, waiting for his bride. Her gaze skated down the line of groomsmen beside him. The last one would be Celine's brother, probably a nerdy-looking guy wearing horn-rimmed glasses, and with a caved-in chest and round shoulders from all that work at a computer.

Except he wasn't one bit like that!

The jolt to her heart was so hard and unexpected, her forward progress almost faltered. Some magical automatic pilot kicked in and kept her going as a wild excitement erupted through her, scrambling her usually sensible mind and staging the dance of the bumble bees in her stomach. Fletcher Stanton was gorgeous. Drop-dead gorgeous. She completely forgot his much-vaunted brain. And his billions. On a purely physical level he was dreamboat material.

He had a hard, masculine, handsome face: strong nose, strong chin, strong cheekbones, straight black brows over thickly lashed dark chocolate eyes, a firmly carved mouth with very sensual lips, hair as black as her own, a cowlick at the side part making it dip attractively over his high, broad forehead. He was the tallest man in the line-up but there was nothing remotely weedy about his body. Every man looked good in a formal dress suit, but his perfectly proportioned physique filled it with superb class.

Her smile must have still been fixed on her face because he smiled at her, revealing a flash of straight white teeth. And was that a sparkle of interest in his eyes? Did he find her attractive? Was he pleased she was his partner for the wedding? Her mind was giddy with hopeful anticipation as she reached the end of the aisle and turned to take her place as the fifth bridesmaid at the side of the altar.

She was definitely looking her best today. Normally she paid very little attention to her appearance apart from being clean and neat, having determined not to let it be of any critical importance to her. Today was different because it was important to fit in with Celine's vision for her wedding.

A beautician had been hired to do everyone's makeup, and Tammy had hardly recognised her own rather ordinary face when she'd finished. Subtle highlighting had made her pansy-violet eyes appear more vivid. Different shades of blusher had lessened the roundness of her cheeks and given colour to her fair skin. Her mouth looked positively lush and dewy—temptingly kissable?— from expertly applied lipstick. As for her slightly tip-tilted nose which had caught the sun all her life, its sprinkle of freckles had been miraculously creamed into non-existence. On top of this, her long hair, usually straight, had been curled into a sexy cascade of loose ringlets by the stylist who'd done all their hair.

She actually *felt* pretty—a strangely new and pleasurable experience, which gave her some inkling of why her mother was obsessed with needing to feel beautiful. And this incredible rush of excitement at having a man as spectacularly handsome as Fletcher Stanton view her with interest…yes, she could see why it might be worth all the trouble. Though it was terribly superficial, she reminded herself, trying not to feel so…unhinged…by the prospect of having this connection with him.

In real terms it was an enforced connection— bridesmaid and groomsman. It wasn't a matter of choice for Fletcher. With his looks and billions, he would have to be accustomed to really beautiful women vying for his attention. *Pretty* probably made their partnering for his sister's wedding more acceptable than if he'd been loaded with someone he found totally unattractive. And she shouldn't forget that Celine *had* called him an arrogant pig, undoubtedly with good reason.

Was it because of his brain or being spoilt for choice where the opposite sex was concerned? Both factors would have to contribute to a sense of superiority compared to the rest of the human race.

Tammy decided not to worry about any of that. He was *hers* for the rest of the day and she was going to make the most of having his company, happily feeding any spark of interest he showed in her. After all, having expected nothing from him, she had nothing to lose. At the very least she would have the novel experience of having the most gorgeous guy here at her side, as well as satisfying her curiosity about him.

The wedding ceremony started and she forced her mind to pay attention to it. Celine deserved her full support—the first of her friends to get married. Maybe I'll be next, she thought, imagining Fletcher in the role of groom. 'To have and to hold from this day forth…' but that was definitely a wild flight of fantasy. She didn't even know the man yet.

Soon…

Celine and Andrew were finally declared husband and wife. The marriage certificate was signed. The organist started playing a triumphant march, and the bride and groom headed the parade back down the aisle, their attendants linking up in turn to follow them. At last Tammy came face-to-face with Fletcher Stanton, and close up he was even more breath-taking. The sheer impact of him made her rush into speech to stiffen up her melting knees.

'Hi! I'm Tammy Haynes.'

He tucked her arm around his and inclined his

tall head to a more intimate angle. 'I know,' he said in a low sexy voice. 'Celine worded me up on you.'

'Uh-oh!' She rolled her eyes, her heart sinking at the many and varied descriptions Celine might have employed in summing her up for her brother—hopefully not the female equivalent of arrogant pig. 'What words did she use?'

He looked amused by her wary tone. 'I was warned that you're a precious friend and I'm to treat you kindly.'

'Well…that's nice.' Relief poured into a smile.

'And I'd better watch what I say to you because in the famous gang of six, you have the smartest mouth.'

Her mouth dropped open in surprise at this, and his gaze slid down to her glistening lips. 'Such a luscious mouth and wit, too,' he drawled teasingly. 'I'm looking forward to getting acquainted with it.'

Tammy scooped in a quick breath and turned her gaze straight ahead while she regained her wits. Fletcher Stanton was scattering them to the winds. All she could think of was how much she wanted to get acquainted with *his* mouth. They'd drawn level with the last pew in the church before she managed a curious thought that had nothing to do with being kissed by him.

'How did you come by the name of Fletcher? It's quite uncommon.'

And rhymed with lecher. Which demonstrated

her mind was still stuck in a sexy groove. Being consumed by lust was a terrible thing. Embarrassing, too, if he was only playing with her.

'My mother was smitten by Marlon Brando's portrayal of Fletcher Christian in the movie of *Mutiny on the Bounty.* She actually loaded me with both names, just as Celine copped Celine Dion after the singer. What parents inflict on their children out of some personal fancy…' His grimace was loaded with nasty memories. 'Why don't they think of what other kids are going to make out of them?'

A stab of shame hit her. She'd just been thinking lecher and no doubt he'd been subjected to that at school. 'What would *you* name your children?' popped out of her mouth. 'If you had them,' she hastily added, not wanting him to think she was fancying the idea of being their mother.

'Paul, Steven, John…' he reeled out with a shrug.

She slid him an arch look. 'No girls' names in there. Aren't they important, too?'

His eyes glittered a challenge. 'Do you like yours?'

Her turn to shrug. 'It's okay. It hasn't brought me any grief.'

One disbelieving eyebrow lifted. 'Wasn't there a TV teen called Tammy who was like an ultra-cute Pollyanna? Your name alone made me think I'd be partnering a bubbly blonde.'

'You'll just have to hang tough if you're disappointed.'

It surprised a short laugh out of him—a laugh that ended in a dazzling grin. 'I'm hanging quite happily, thank you.'

She bet he was well hung, too.

Tammy struggled to lift her mind off how he might look naked.

'Actually my name is Tamalyn, though most people call me Tam or Tammy,' she said off-handedly.

'Ah! Now that does suit you. It has an exotic ring to it.'

Exotic? Her heart fluttered. Was that his impression of her? It had to be the mass of curls giving her a different look. If he saw her tomorrow when her hair would be straight again… But today was today and she wasn't about to belittle what impact she had made on *this* man. In fact, she seized on the exotic theme and ran with it.

'Tama is the Native-American word for thunderbolt,' she informed him with a flirty little smile. 'My mother added Lyn to feminise it.'

'Thunderbolt…' His mouth twitched in amusement. 'Am I in danger of being struck down?'

'Only if you don't treat me kindly.'

He laughed.

Bubbles of exhilaration bounced around her brain as they emerged from the church. Fletcher was enjoying her company. He thought her exotic. Life was beautiful. The sun was not only shining on the bride but also on her fifth bridesmaid.

There was virtually no chance of any further personal conversation while the wedding photographer kept posing them on the church steps, demanding they move here and there for different group shots, though she didn't mind when he insisted they press closer and Fletcher's arm curled around her waist, drawing her into standing against him.

She'd always considered herself of average height, yet he was so tall, her head only reached the top of his shoulder. It gave her a lovely, warm sense of having a big strong man to look after her, which, of course, was what women had wanted in primitive societies. Fletcher Stanton was definitely striking lots of primitive chords in her.

'Mmm…exotic perfume, too,' he murmured close to her ear, making it tingle with the waft of his breath.

'White Diamonds,' she told him, glad that Jennifer had insisted on dabbing some of the expensive scent on her.

His eyes twinkled wickedly. 'Sounds cold. Should be called Purple Passion.'

She giggled. Couldn't help herself. Couldn't stop.

Jennifer shot her a quizzical look. 'What's so funny?'

'Nothing,' Tammy spluttered, shaking her head as she tried to regain control of her behaviour.

'Come on, give,' her friend urged, casting a curious look at Fletcher.

'I think Tamalyn is having a purple day,' he said with mock gravity.

'Tamalyn?' Jennifer's eyes widened incredulously at the rarely spoken name.

'No, no, it's a golden day. Pure gold,' Tammy rattled out, bursting into giggles again.

Fletcher squeezed her waist. She hoped it meant happy agreement with her correction and not an act of exasperation with her hilarity, which had probably destroyed her exotic mystique. But Purple Passion was too over the top and *golden* described this situation perfectly, as long as Fletcher had a sense of humour.

'You can tell us the joke in the limo,' Jennifer said, eyes flashing insistently. 'We're moving on now.'

So they were, Celine and Andrew heading down the church steps to their car, guests throwing rice at them. The bridesmaids were to return to the limousine which had brought them to the church, the groomsmen travelling separately in theirs to Boronia House which had been booked for the reception. Having sobered up from her fit of giggles, she flashed Fletcher a smile as she reluctantly stepped out of his hold.

'See you at the next stop.'

'I'm looking forward to it,' he replied, his eyes simmering with the promise of more fun and games with her.

Tammy floated on a cloud of delight as she followed her friends down the steps. She and Fletcher were definitely connecting. The attraction was mutual. There had been no sign at all of him being an arrogant pig and she couldn't imagine why Celine had described him in such terms. Maybe it was a sibling thing—little sister overshadowed by older brother who was outstandingly successful in his field.

But Celine had also said he offended people and she surely wouldn't be wrong about that, given their long family history together. It was possible, because it was his sister's wedding, he had taken her warning to treat his partner kindly to heart and was going out of his way not to offend. Whatever… it was too soon for Tammy to make any judgement on this. Besides, the buoyant happiness she was feeling was too good to question right now.

Go with it, girl, she told herself, and was grinning her pleasure in the situation as she piled into the bridesmaids' limousine with her friends. They were no sooner on their way than they all turned their focus on her.

'Wow! Did you get the prize!' Kirsty started. 'I'm with the best man but he sure isn't the best!'

'Yeah…lucky you, Tam!' Hannah chimed in with blatant envy. 'Never mind the billions he's made, that guy is hot, hot, hot!'

'How come Celine never told us her brother was such a fabulous hunk, always calling him the brain?' Lucy complained.

'He can't be too nerdy in the brain department because he was making Tammy laugh her head off,' Jennifer informed them before quizzing her directly. 'What was he saying to you? And why did he call you Tamalyn? Were you being uppity with him?'

'He thinks I'm exotic, so I was giving him exotic,' she answered.

They all hooted at this description of her.

'Don't knock it!' she commanded. 'It's not every day I look like this, or smell like this, thank you, Jennifer—so I might as well take advantage of it.'

'Go for it, girl!' they chorussed, echoing what she'd told herself.

They'd always encouraged each other with that phrase. It was characteristic of the camaraderie they shared. Tammy thought how lucky she had been to have such good friends over the years, and hoped their closeness would not get too eroded by other relationships. Now that Celine had Andrew, she wasn't so available to them anymore, which was natural enough. As each of them got married— if they did—the degree of separation would inevitably become greater. Life moved on. She just hoped it wouldn't move them too far apart.

Fletcher's world revolved around the serious hubs of power overseas, a whole ocean away from Sydney and the life she had mapped out for herself. It was a point she would do well to remember, not get too carried away by an attraction that had little chance of going any further than today.

Yet who knew what the future held?

Right now it held Fletcher Stanton at the next stop, and all she wanted to do was bask in that wonderfully tantalising thought.

CHAPTER TWO

THE grounds of Boronia House were picture perfect: wonderful old pine trees shading glorious banks of azaleas in full bloom. The house itself was a lovely backdrop, built in the old colonial style with verandahs running around both storeys, tall French doors opening onto them, white columns interspersing the intricately patterned white iron lace that ran around the eaves and the upper balcony. In the centre of the manicured lawn was a magnolia tree, laden with its purple and pink flowers, the grass around it strewn with fallen petals. The photographer had just posed the bride and groom in front of it when Fletcher Stanton started tarnishing his golden image.

'That looks so romantic!' Tammy enthused with a happy sigh.

'Yes. I'd have to give Celine top marks for picking great staging,' he agreed amiably. 'But I can't help questioning if the romance of a wedding has clouded her brain.'

They were alone together, waiting in the shade of a giant pine tree for the next group photo-call. The others had trooped off to the house to refresh themselves while they were free to do so. Tammy had not been inclined to leave Fletcher's side, eager to share every moment she could with him, and he had remained with her, apparently just as pleased to have her company.

However, the cynical twist of his last comment was not to her liking. She turned to him with a frown. 'What do you mean?'

He shrugged. 'Celine is only twenty-three, not even set in a career. It's stupid to get married this young.' His eyes challenged hers, cutting through the shock of his statement. 'Would *you* do it?'

'If I loved a man to distraction, as Celine does Andrew, and he loved me just as deeply, yes, I would,' she answered vehemently.

One black eyebrow arched. 'You'd tie yourself to a relationship before you've even begun to explore all you're capable of? Before you find out what else you might want in your life?'

It came over loud and clear that *he* was not about to tie himself to a relationship that might cramp his life style.

'I don't see why marriage has to stop anything,' she argued. 'It should complement things. Make them even better with sharing.'

'How often does marriage live up to that ideal?' he mocked.

Never when it's entered into for the wrong reasons, Tammy thought.

'The statistics tell another story,' Fletcher ran on, arrogantly confident of his argument. 'Especially where *young* marriages are concerned.'

Young…old… Tammy had seen absolute devotion to each other in all sorts of couples during her time in different hospital wards, training to be a nurse. Marriage could and did work if there was real caring between the persons involved.

'I happen to think that letting statistics rule your life is even more stupid,' she retorted hotly, delivering a scathing look before refixing her gaze on Celine and Andrew, who were looking adoringly at each other for the camera. Though it wasn't just for the camera, Tammy assured herself. Their feelings were real, not manufactured for this moment.

'There are always exceptions to any rule,' she added to drive the point home, wanting the best for her friend. The very best. And it was offensive for Fletcher to be airing these opinions at his own sister's wedding. He should try having a bit more faith in Celine's judgement. Soul-mates were difficult to find and age had nothing to do with it.

Regrettably, Fletcher Stanton was taking himself

out of the running to be her soul-mate. Vexation and disappointment tore at Tammy's heart. He'd looked so good, felt so good, sounded good until a minute ago.

'That's true,' he conceded, re-animating her interest in him.

There was nothing too arrogant about a man who would stand corrected. She could deal with a reasonable human being. The rigidity in her spine softened. Her ears tingled with anticipation for what more he might say, preferably something she could hug warmly to her heart.

'I do hope this marriage doesn't turn into a mistake. I want Celine to be happy in it.'

The sincerity in his voice was lovely to hear, and Tammy was deeply in tune with these sentiments. 'I've never seen her so happy,' she said, smiling dreamily at the newly joined couple.

'What about you, Tamalyn? Are you happy with your life?'

She turned the smile to him. 'Yes, I am.' As long as she didn't count not being in love with anyone. Though a wild hope whispered that could change by the end of the evening. 'I'm now a fully qualified nurse, and this year I'm training to be a midwife which is what I want to be.'

'A midwife...' He eyed her curiously. 'Why?'

'Because there's nothing more exciting than

helping to deliver a new life. I love working in the maternity ward.'

He looked bemused. 'You don't mind squawling babies?'

'They only cry when something's not right for them. I like making things right. It's very rewarding.'

'I guess that's relatively easy to do when their needs are so basic,' he said thoughtfully. 'Needs get much more complex as people get older.'

'How complex are yours?'

The quick shot surprised him. He broke into a peal of laughter, his eyes dancing wickedly as he eventually answered, 'Oh, mine are very basic right now. Not the least bit complex.'

Her toes curled.

Lust was looking at her straight in the face. Lust was rushing through her own body. He was so devilishly handsome, so very desirable, it was madly exhilarating to have him desiring her, too. But a hardy strain of common sense reminded her he would probably be flying back to the other side of the world after the wedding and he could be viewing her as a handy one-night stand, whereas she would want a night of intimacy between them to be the beginning of a relationship that had more going for it than just sex.

She wondered if she could be a midwife in other countries.

Or whether he might settle back here. After all, today's technology made everything and everyone readily accessible. The magazine article had mentioned that one of his team of wizards lived in Canberra. Surely Fletcher could base himself in Sydney if he wanted to.

'What are you working on now?' she asked.

He shrugged. 'Basically hackwork. Making adjustments to the system to satisfy our clients' requirements.'

'You sound bored by it.'

'Like changing babies' nappies,' he tossed at her with a teasing grin. 'I enjoy being in on the creative process, just as you do. The birth of new ideas, new ways of attacking problems, is very exciting. But the run-of-the-mill stuff—a repetitive task that has to be done—it doesn't raise a tingle in the mind, does it?'

Clever…linking it to her life. Was he patronising her? Would a genius really be interested in a nurse, apart from on a physical level?

'Do you have any females on your technology team?'

He shook his head. 'All men.'

'No meeting of minds with a woman,' she muttered, then flushed at having spoken such a revealing thought out loud.

'On the contrary, I'm finding considerable pleasure in meeting yours. And connecting with it.'

Her flush deepened as heat raced around her bloodstream. Did he mean it or was he playing with her?

'Tammy!'

Celine's call distracted her from pursuing the question. She turned to her friend who was beckoning action.

'Bring Fletcher over here and let the photographer pose you two in front of the magnolia. It should be a marvellous shot with your mauve dress. We can get it done before the others come back.'

'Must oblige the bride,' Fletcher murmured, instantly hooking her arm around his and leading her over to be posed with him.

Tammy couldn't help revelling in being close to him again, measuring her own slight but very feminine figure against his powerful male physique as the photographer pressed them together, feeling the warmth of Fletcher's arm around her waist, wondering what it would be like to have both his arms around her. There was to be dancing after the reception dinner. She would know then.

The wedding group returned in force and there was little opportunity for more really personal conversation during the rest of the photo shoot. Her friends were full of chatter, and their partners claimed Fletcher's attention. The wedding guests arrived and were ushered out onto the top balcony of the house where they were served drinks and canapes as they socialised and watched the action in the grounds below, applauding the more novel poses, like the one of the five bridesmaids circling the bride with hands linked.

'Very pretty,' Fletcher remarked on that particular arrangement, his mouth quirking as he added, 'Though I've never thought of Celine as a maypole.'

Tammy rolled her eyes at this ridiculous interpretation before setting him straight. 'Today she is the star of our gang of six, and the rest of us were paying homage to her.'

'Homage...because she got married?' He looked incredulous. 'Is that the ultimate peak of ambition for you and your friends?'

The hint of scorn in his voice stung her into a sharp reply. 'Marriage is generally considered a huge milestone in one's life, like birth and death...'

'And divorce,' he slid in.

'Do you have to be so negative?' she snapped.

'I'm a realist.' One black eyebrow lifted in challenge. 'I thought you would be, too. Nursing might be a noble profession but it can't leave you with too many illusions about people.'

'You're right. You see the best and the worst and everything in between, which gives me all the more reason to respect the best, to pay homage to it and celebrate it.'

So, criticise that at your peril! she mentally shot at him.

'You think Celine now has the best…something you aspire to?' he shot back at her.

He made it sound as though she and her friends were a bunch of empty-headed girls whose only goal in life was to get married. Okay, they might hope for it, wish for it, dream about it, but none of them thought it an *ultimate ambition*. It would only be good if they met the right guy, and Celine was certain Andrew was *the one*.

'*She* believes it's the best for her and I'm not about to put that down.'

It was a warning for him to stop doing it.

He didn't, coming straight back with 'How on earth could Celine know what's best for her when she's only twenty-three?'

Harping on her age again…being so superior with his older experience!

Tammy eyed him disdainfully. 'What does knowledge have to do with it? Choosing a mate is more about instinct. Maybe all that brain work you do has choked off your instincts. You think too much and don't trust natural feelings.'

He smirked. 'If you're talking about biological urges…'

He had *them* all right, and Tammy knew they were directed at her, but she wasn't feeling so thrilled about that right now. In fact, she was downright offended that he had reduced her argument to nothing more than lust. 'Instinct covers more ground than basic biological urges,' she stated bitingly.

'It starts with chemistry,' he insisted.

He wasn't taking her view onboard, wasn't even giving it respect.

'Well, let me tell you chemistry can be very swiftly switched off by other out-of-tune elements.'

He grinned. 'Celine was right. You do have a smart mouth.'

'She was right about you, too. You *are* arrogant, thinking you know better than everyone else.'

And before she could regret delivering that knock-out blow with her smart mouth, she tossed her head in the air and turned her back on him, walking off to place herself in the company of her like-minded friends. Where she stayed, for the rest of the time before the reception dinner, pointedly ignoring him, feeling strongly it was a matter of loyalty. She would not side with him against her friends, even if he was drop-dead gorgeous. The hormones he had stimulated could gallop as much as they liked. They were heading nowhere.

It was a relief when they finally sat down at the long wedding-party table and he was at the other end of it, out of sight and out of any possible contact—physical and verbal. Nevertheless, she found it difficult to get him out of her mind, despite chatting almost feverishly with her fellow bridesmaids. They, of course, wanted to know how it was going with Fletcher, but she dismissed that very firmly.

'Forget it! The brain took over from the body and it wasn't to my liking. Hunk is not everything!'

They ruefully agreed with this declaration and the subject was dropped. There was so much else to comment on: the wedding decor, the dressing of the guests, the food, the speeches—which Tammy privately decided Fletcher would consider a whole lot of sentimental claptrap, but which she thought were beautifully heartfelt and heart touching.

She smiled, clapped, laughed in all the right places, though no matter how hard she tried to enjoy herself, there was this weird leaden weight on her heart—something she'd never felt before, not over a man. Fletcher had stirred a lot of new feelings in her today. Had she been too hasty in taking such decisive umbrage against him? Was this the weight of disappointment because he wasn't how she'd wanted him to be, or of regret for cutting herself off before exploring the experience further?

Fortunately, when the bridal party all trooped off to the powder room before the cutting of the cake, Celine cleared up some of the turmoil in Tammy's mind.

'Did I detect something going on between you

and my brother, Tammy?' she asked with a little frown of concern.

'Just a bit of flirtation. You didn't tell me he was so handsome.'

Celine grimaced. 'Alpha male at its best and worst—that's Fletcher. Didn't he put you off with his supposedly superior intellect?'

Tammy shrugged. 'I had to cut him down a few times.'

'Well, I'm glad to hear you're not completely bowled over by him. Fletcher is only into very casual relationships, and I *mean* casual. No woman is good enough to keep his interest. Besides which he flies back to London on Monday. He'll be out of your life before you even begin to know him properly.'

'No problem,' Tammy answered airily and concentrated on renewing her lipstick, telling herself to stop maundering over what might have been with Fletcher Stanton. He was definitely *not* the right man for her.

Her body, however, staged a highly unsettling rebellion against that edict when she had to dance with him.

The bridal waltz followed the cutting of the cake. The bridesmaids and groomsmen were scheduled to join in after Celine's and Andrew's showpiece solo performance. There was no avoiding it. As the fifth bridesmaid, Tammy had to line up with the fifth groomsman. They stood together, waiting for their turn to step onto the floor, Tammy looking studiously ahead, acutely aware that her pulse was racing and her female hormones were zinging into a merry dance of their own at the prospect of physical connection with the man beside her.

'Ready?' he asked.

She glanced up and caught a devilish twinkle in his dark eyes. 'I hope you can waltz,' she answered, trying to dampen the rush of heat through her bloodstream.

'Counting one, two, three, is not beyond me' was his sardonic reply.

'Mathematical skill does not guarantee a natural rhythm,' she instantly countered, bristling at his arrogance again. 'Some people have it. Some don't.'

'Do you have it?'

'Yes.'

'Then we should move well together,' he said with such sexy satisfaction, Tammy told herself to keep her smart mouth shut because it was only giving him ammunition to light a fire she had to put out.

This attraction was going nowhere.

She was not going to be a casual, meaningless one-night stand for Fletcher Stanton. Pride forbade it. She deserved more from a man than to be left to herself after an intimate connection.

'Our turn now,' he said, and swept her onto the

dance floor, one arm clamping her lower body to his, his powerful thighs pushing hers into the slow sensual rhythm of 'Moon River,' the jazz waltz Celine had chosen.

He held her so closely, her breasts pressed to his chest, she had to put her arm up around his neck, and he didn't just hold her other hand. He intertwined their fingers, fueling the hot sense he was claiming possession of her and had no intention of letting go. Tammy couldn't stop herself from virtually melting into him. He danced divinely. Never had she had such a masterful partner. The question started raging through her mind—what would he be like in bed?

Mercifully the music stopped and she pulled herself back from the brink of floating into dangerous places with Fletcher Stanton. 'I have to go and serve cake now,' she said, demanding release.

'It can wait. The other guests have just been invited to join us on the dance floor,' he argued, his eyes simmering with temptations that had to be denied or she might end up where she was determined not to be.

'Many of them won't. It's the bridesmaids' duty to take around trays of cake,' she stated categorically.

'How many more duties do you have to perform tonight?'

'This is the last one,' she had to admit.

'Good! Then I'll catch up with you after it's done.'

He slowly untwined his hand from hers and removed his arm from around her waist, his dark gaze holding hers with an intensity of purpose that sent little shivers down her spine. She took a deep breath, knowing she had to make a fighting stand.

'This was a duty dance, you know. I don't have to do anything more with you.'

'But we have such perfect rhythm together. Why deny the pleasure of pursuing it further?'

Because it was a straight-out case of dancing with the devil. But Tammy couldn't say that since it would reveal how tempted she was.

'What's your favourite dance?' he pressed.

'The salsa,' she answered, half hoping he couldn't do it, half wanting him to be brilliant at it because she loved it so much.

He grinned with wicked confidence. 'I'll salsa you off your feet.'

'Maybe. Maybe not,' she said archly, trying her utmost to stay cool. 'Please excuse me. Duty calls.'

She could feel his eyes burning into her back as she walked away. He was a terribly sexy beast. Could she risk the excitement of doing the salsa with him? Better not. No doubt it would tease more lustful desires, and she might not feel strong enough to resist them.

As it turned out she found the best possible

excuse to escape any pursuit from Fletcher for the rest of the evening. Celine's ten-year-old cousin, Ryan, had disgraced himself, surreptitiously drinking alcohol, throwing up and feeling wretched. Tammy offered to sit with him on the downstairs verandah so his parents could continue enjoying their niece's wedding reception. Knowing she was a qualified nurse, they were happily relieved to let her take care of him.

Ryan curled up on her lap and dropped off to sleep. Tammy was grateful for the cool night air. It helped dispel the feverish physical yearning that had almost pulled her down a very stupid course. Hadn't she learnt from her mother's life that rich arrogant men didn't stick around after they'd got what they wanted? Fletcher Stanton wouldn't be any different. His own sister had spelled that out. If she let her deeply set principles be swept aside by his powerful attraction, she'd be disgusted with herself when he flew away on Monday.

Attraction for men like him was a very temporary thing. If she hadn't looked *exotic* today, would he have shown any interest in her, felt any desire for her? Tammy doubted it. She didn't understand why she'd felt such a strong connection to him. The feeling couldn't be trusted, anyway. Better to set it aside than risk her heart on a man who had such a cynical view of love and marriage—a man who wasn't looking for anything more than casual sex with a woman.

Ryan's parents came to collect him when the bride was about to leave. Tammy joined the other bridesmaids just in time for the throwing of the bouquet. Kirsty caught it. They all laughingly trailed after the bride and groom, making their exit from Boronia House. Fletcher caught up with her outside where the limousines were lined up, ready to transport their designated passengers.

'Where have you been?' he demanded, frustrated at having his desires thwarted by her absence.

'Looking after a sick guest,' she answered, thrusting out a hand to him for a coolly formal farewell. 'Goodbye, Fletcher. I hope you have a smooth flight back to London on Monday.'

The finality in her voice triggered a savage glitter of mockery in his eyes. 'I take it you're on duty again tomorrow.'

'Yes,' she said firmly.

He wasn't used to rejection, didn't like it, but it was clearly beneath him to fight it. He cloaked himself with an unprickable air of arrogance as he took her hand, enveloping it in the heat and strength of his, making it feel small and fragile— too little for him—everything she was…too little to take him on.

'It was a pleasure meeting you, Tamalyn,' he rolled

out with the same cool politeness she had dealt to him, then surprised her by sardonically adding, 'Thunderbolts don't come my way very often.'

It was on the tip of her tongue to say he probably needed more of them to puncture his arrogance on a regular basis. She clamped down on the comment, not wanting to be provocative at this point. He was going away. There was no future for her with Celine's brother. His life was elsewhere. But despite all her sensible reasoning, the leaden weight was back on her heart.

'Another time. Another place. Who knows? We might strike each other again,' she replied, determinedly wriggling her hand free so she could leave.

His eyes bored into hers, striking hard right now. 'It's a waste…not using the present.'

'Nothing's a waste…if you learn from it,' she said back. 'Life is one long experience and meeting you today has been part of it. Thank you and goodbye, Fletcher.'

She turned away before regret at not having the experience of going to bed with him could tear at her conviction that it would be wrong for her.

She was only twenty-three.

The promise of one night with Fletcher Stanton was not enough to compromise her ideals on how a relationship between a man and woman should work.

CHAPTER THREE

The Second Wedding

Was Fletcher Stanton going to be there?

The question was like a squirrel on a treadmill running through Tammy's mind. Had been for months. Ever since Kirsty had announced her engagement to Paul Hathaway and it came out in conversation that Paul's brother, Max, was the mathematical super-brain in Canberra who was an integral member of Fletcher's high-tech team. Which was one of those coincidences in life that seemed to make the world very small.

A close professional connection didn't mean a social one, Tammy had told herself a hundred times. Even if Fletcher and Max Hathaway were friends as well as colleagues, Paul was based in Sydney, an IT specialist for an international bank with his own circle of friends to invite to the wedding. It was highly unlikely that a brother's friend who lived and worked overseas would be invited to the wedding.

Of course, the question could have been settled once and for all if she'd simply asked Kirsty if Fletcher's name was on the Hathaways' confirmed guest list, but she hadn't been able to bring herself to do it. There was something really pathetic about showing an interest in a man who had not pursued any interest in her beyond the one encounter at Celine's wedding, and that had been six months ago.

Though she had rejected him.

Very pointedly.

What man would pursue a woman after that?

He probably hadn't even returned to Australia since then.

Sometimes she cursed having met Fletcher Stanton at all. Regardless of everything that had been wrong about him, he'd made too big an impact on her to forget. The memory of the sexual chemistry which had sizzled between them still bothered her. Other men she'd dated over the years—nice men, good guys—had never lit that spark in her. Nor had she ever felt challenged by them in any vital way.

She *wanted* to meet Fletcher again, needed to settle this crazy sense of missing out on something only he could supply. Just a bit of personal contact could stop this endless torment. If he didn't stir her hormones with the same wild excitement, if he was too rudely arrogant to bother with…maybe then she would stop the stupid habit of taking out the photograph of the two of them together in front of the magnolia tree at Celine's wedding and fretting over what might have been a bad decision to close the door on him.

She felt almost sick with nervous tension, the morning of the wedding. As she travelled in the city train across the harbour to the eastern suburbs where the others all lived, she told herself to stop thinking of him, focus on her friends, be happy for Kirsty. The gang was to meet at a hairdressing salon in Bondi Junction and she had to be as high-spirited as the rest of them were bound to be. It was a big day—the second wedding—and Fletcher should not be a factor in that.

She was the last to arrive.

And walked straight in on Kirsty saying, 'Oh, I forgot to tell you at our hens' party last night, Celine. Your brother's coming to the wedding.'

'Fletcher?'

The shock in Celine's voice was mirrored on her face as she swivelled around in her chair to question Kirsty…and caught sight of Tammy, her feet stopped dead at the reception desk as she desperately tried to keep her expression blank.

'Tam…' Celine grimaced. 'Did you hear that?'

'What?' she asked, pretending ignorance, hoping the wild pumping of her heart would not shoot a tell-tale flush up her neck.

The rest of the gang was already in the salon. They all looked at her, watching for her reaction. Were they remembering her connection with Fletcher at Celine's wedding? Had they guessed that *he* was the reason for her lack of any enthusiastic interest in other guys in recent times? Tammy squirmed inside as she waited what seemed like aeons for Celine to answer.

It was Kirsty who finally broke the news. 'Fletcher asked Max if he could come to the wedding.'

Celine turned to her, stunned anew. 'He *asked* him?'

'E-mailed the request on Thursday,' Kirsty explained.

'How extraordinary!' Celine shook her head in disbelief. 'I didn't know he was home. Mum didn't tell me.'

'Max said he'd be flying in this morning,' Kirsty went on.

'Pushing himself in when he hasn't been invited. That's not like Fletcher,' Celine remarked, frowning.

Kirsty shrugged dismissively. 'An extra guest doesn't matter. It's only finger food at the reception, no set tables.'

Celine shot a concerned glance at Tammy who

was being ushered to the chair beside Jennifer's, then questioned Kirsty further. 'Did Max say why he wanted to come?'

'Not that I know of. He called Paul, made the request, and Paul passed it on to me. Just said Fletcher was flying in this morning and wanted to attend the wedding.'

Jennifer grinned at Tammy as she sat down next to her, eyes twinkling teasingly. 'You might get another chance at him, Tam. He was quite put out when you disappeared on him last time, asking around for you.'

'That was half a year ago,' Tammy reminded her, trying to ignore the sudden kick to her heart. 'And I gave him the flick, remember?'

'He *was* interested in you, though,' Lucy argued. 'He might have mellowed since then, not be so arrogant. I hate to see such a gorgeous hunk go to waste.'

'Oh, stop it, Lucy!' Celine shot at her. 'Fletcher runs through women like there's an endless supply of them. Chasing after him would be the worst thing Tam could do.'

Lucy, irrepressible as always, rolled her eyes in sexy suggestiveness. 'Not if she catches him. I reckon he'd be worth crawling into bed with.'

Hannah backed her up. 'I thought he was hot, too. If he looked my way, I'd be seriously tempted.'

Having had enough time to recover some equilibrium, Tammy drily stated, 'I'm sure he only looked my way because I was dolled up for Celine's wedding.'

'Well, you're going to be dolled up again today for mine,' Kirsty pointed out.

'So why not make the most of it?' Lucy pressed. 'If I had that gorgeous hunk panting over me, I'd ignore the brain above the belt and engage the one below it.'

'And what would that get me?' Tam sliced at her. 'He lives overseas.'

'Quite possibly a climactic moment of pleasure you could treasure forever.' Lucy slanted her a quizzical look. 'Ever had one, Tam? A really mind-blowing one? You never talk about your sex life. You just listen to us.'

'Guess I find yours more interesting. And yes, I have had a few mind-blowing moments.'

With Fletcher Stanton when he danced the waltz with me.

It wasn't what Lucy meant, but that was still the highlight of Tammy's sex life. She'd never been able to adopt the free and easy attitude her friends had towards what they considered a natural connection between a man and a woman. To her, physical intimacy had to go hand in hand with love. She didn't want to give herself for less.

'Well, that's a relief!' Lucy declared. 'I always thought you never let your hair down enough.'

'It's down right now,' Tammy retorted, waving to the hair-stylist who was standing behind her chair and running the long black tresses through her fingers. 'How do you want it done, Kirsty?'

The subject of Fletcher was dropped in favour of the more important and immediate aim to get everything right for the wedding. Kirsty wanted Tammy's hair swept around to one side of her face and curled down over her shoulder. Very feminine, but was it sexy, Tammy wondered, secretly hoping Fletcher would be attracted to her again, wanting close contact, needing to test her feelings towards him.

The bridesmaids' dresses were in a sort of Grecian style. Made in pure silk satin chiffon, the rouched bodice and soft princess-line skirt were constructed in different shades of blue from sky to royal, and the dress was virtually backless, plunging to below the waistline. That was definitely sexy, baring the whole curve of her spine.

Did Fletcher's impulse to attend the wedding have anything to do with her?

He had to know she'd be one of Kirsty's bridesmaids, given his informed comment on *the famous gang of six* at Celine's wedding.

Did he remember her as strongly as she remembered him?

In Tammy's nerve-twittering state, the hours until the wedding seemed endless. From the hair-dressing salon they moved on to Beautiful Nails for the perfect manicure and pedicure, then to Kirsty's parents' house at Bellevue Hill for a late lunch and the rest of the preparations.

A make-up artist was booked to come in and do their faces, and surveying the brilliant job done on her own, Tammy wryly reflected that Fletcher would be seeing her at her superficial best again. Would he have found her attractive *au naturelle?* She felt their connection had gone more than skin deep, but wasn't so sure of that on his side.

At last the cars arrived to take them to the wedding venue. Kirsty had chosen to be married in the national park, right on the South Head of the Harbour, the open-air ceremony to be held as the sun was lowering in the sky, shedding a golden light over the great arch of the bridge, the opera house and the long stretch of the harbour with its myriad coves and bays—a spectacular backdrop. A heritage house, situated in the park, had been turned into a function centre where the reception would take place.

It wasn't a long drive from Bellevue Hill. Tammy was too choked up with tense anticipation to chat with her friends. She mentally ticked off the landmarks they passed—the Vaucluse Yacht Club,

Fisherman's Wharf, Camp Cove, Lady Bay Beach which was famous for being one of the earliest nudists' beaches in Sydney—each one bringing her closer to Fletcher Stanton and her chance to make contact with him.

Her heart quickened to a wild flutter as the cars pulled up on a long driveway which ran in front of the two-storeyed brick house and above the landscaped terrace where guests were milling amongst the rows of chairs set out for the ceremony. There were too many people for her to spot Fletcher straight away, and she didn't have time to give more than a cursory glance at the crowd. Her friends were piling out of the car and she had to follow, carry through her bridesmaid role for Kirsty who looked wonderful in her own Grecian style gown.

A flight of stone steps led down to the terrace. The harpist Kirsty had hired for the ceremony was positioned at the head of them and the guests settled as he started playing his magnificent gold concert harp, instantly creating a romantic atmosphere for the wedding. The five bridesmaids lined up beside him, ready for the walk down the steps.

Celine was behind Tammy, and she leaned forward and muttered, 'Fletcher did come. I can hardly believe it. But there he is, standing beside Andrew at the back of the seated guests and he's staring straight at you.'

Tammy's head instantly swivelled to where Celine had directed, her pulse racing in excitement at this possible evidence that Fletcher might still be interested in her.

Her swinging gaze caught his and for several electric moments, Tammy was transfixed by a bolting sense of joy. He didn't look away. The distance between them was too great for her to see the expression in his eyes but she *felt* their laser-like strength of purpose, probing for a response from her. *Yes, yes, yes,* flew wildly round her mind. She should have smiled, she thought afterwards, given a positive physical signal, but before her mind could come down from its high to reason sensibly, Celine poked her in the back and hissed, 'Move!'

Her attention jerked back to performing her bridesmaid role. Hannah was already on the third step down, Lucy on the top one. She had to move forward, keep two steps between each bridesmaid. *And* watch her footing. The stone slabs dipped a bit in the middle, worn down by innumerable people treading on them during the long naval history of this place. There would be time for Fletcher later.

The wedding procession rounded the stone fountain in the middle of the lower terrace, then turned to walk down the makeshift aisle to the right of it, heading for where the groom and his men were lined up beside the celebrant. Tammy could barely stop her feet from dancing. Walking at a measured pace was an act of stern discipline. But it was easy to smile. In fact, she couldn't wipe the smile off her face for the entire ceremony.

She was still smiling when Fletcher made his way to her as other guests crowded around the bride and groom to congratulate them. Her heart was pounding with nervous excitement as she watched him deliberately target her and home in.

'Tamalyn…'

Her name sounded like a drum-roll coming from deep within his throat. His dark eyes seemed to burn into her soul. A wave of heat rushed through her. She clutched her bouquet tightly as though it was the only support system she had to hold herself together. It was important to stay alert, to assess where Fletcher was coming from and what he wanted of her.

'Hi!' she said in warm welcome. 'I didn't think weddings were your thing, Fletcher. What are you doing here?'

'Fate took a hand in this one with Kirsty marrying Max's brother,' he answered smoothly, smiling over the coincidence, not mentioning how he'd used it. 'And may I say it was worth coming, just to see you again.'

'I'll take that as a compliment,' she said lightly, wary of actually believing that seeing her was his only purpose behind this visit. He might have business with Max Hathaway after the wedding.

'I mean it,' he insisted in his deep sexy voice. 'Each time we meet your beauty hits me like a thunderbolt.'

The words gave her a queazy, defensive feeling. Beauty had no holding power. Her mother's life proved that. And how Fletcher had seen her at both weddings was very temporary, manufactured for the occasion. She didn't want it to be her main attraction for him, instinctively bridling against it.

'Ah! But the strike is like a flash in the pan, Fletcher,' she said with an ironic twist. 'You recover and move on.'

'I carry the memory with me. And the scars.'

'Scars?' She arched quizzical eyebrows, wanting to know if she really had deeply affected him.

'Battle wounds.' He made a wry grimace. 'I came off losing with you last time.'

Tammy eyed him warily. Was this approach to her an ego thing? 'Does that mean that you're out to win today?' she asked.

'Do I have a chance?'

'That probably depends on how much you offend me.'

'I've learnt my lesson,' he said with mock gravity. 'No comments on your friends' marriages.'

'You *can* say good things,' she suggested, wishing for a change of attitude on his part.

'I'd rather concentrate on you.' His eyes burned into hers with an intensity of purpose that would not accept any evasion. 'Are you connected to anyone, Tamalyn?'

A man, he meant. Tammy instantly seized the opportunity to clear that deck both ways.

'No. Are you?'

He smiled, the intensity relaxing into a simmer of satisfaction. 'I came alone. I hoped to have the pleasure of your company this evening.'

The pleasure of her company...

A flood of warmth invaded her heart, soothing the troubled need to be a person he valued for more than her physical attraction. It emboldened her enough to tease him. 'Pleasure, Fletcher? You must be a masochist, since you carry wounds from our previous encounter.'

He laughed, delight in her response lighting up his face. 'I find the battle with you envigorating.'

'Then I'll try to be at my challenging best whenever you seek me out.'

'As soon as you're finished with your bridesmaid's duties, I'll be at your side.'

'Eager for the lash of my smart tongue?'

The provocative comment ignited a blaze of desire in his eyes. 'It's an addictive taste,' he said, his gaze dropping to her mouth.

He meant to kiss her tonight. No doubt about

that. And she wanted him to, wanted him to so badly that her body signalled a wild urge to let it happen. Her breasts tingled, her nipples tightening into hard buds, her heart thumped into a gallop, her stomach contracted and every nerve in her body buzzed. She was too choked up to speak.

Jennifer's call broke the tension-filled moment. 'Tammy, photographs.'

'Got to go.'

The words came out in a guttural jerk. She swallowed hard, needing to work some moisture down her throat.

His gaze flicked up. 'I'll patiently watch you perform for the camera,' he drawled, a sensual promise in the slow movement of his mouth.

'Don't miss the background view,' she tossed at him. 'It might remind you there's more spectacular beauty right here on Sydney Harbour than anywhere else in the world.'

And she wanted him to be homesick for it, wanted him to be sick with yearning for her, too. As she walked over to her friends, she fiercely hoped that whatever pleasures they shared tonight would burn into Fletcher Stanton's heart so deeply, she'd be the only woman he wanted in his life.

CHAPTER FOUR

FLETCHER zeroed in on her again the moment the photographic session was over, with one of the waiters in tow, ensuring she had her choice from a tray of canapes and handing her a glass of champagne.

'Shall we find a quiet spot where we can enjoy the view together?' he suggested, his eyes transmitting pleasure in her—warm, blood-tingling pleasure.

The groomsman partnering her had a girlfriend amongst the guests so she felt no social obligation to remain with him. Nor was she needed for any further bridesmaid duty until much later this evening. Free to please herself, Tammy had no hesitation in agreeing to Fletcher's plan. She wanted to be alone with him, wanted to explore what he made her feel.

'Lead the way,' she invited.

He curled a protective arm around her waist as he negotiated their way through the crowd and

Tammy found herself once again revelling in the sense of dominant strength keeping her safe, taking care of her. The male-female connection felt very intense, as though they were locked in step together, moving in a capsule of space that was uniquely theirs—a capsule permeated with acute sexual awareness.

He took her down a short flight of stone steps to a lower terrace where several park benches were placed to catch the long-range vista of the harbour. His arm dropped away from her as he saw her seated. He hooked it on the back of the bench, seating himself beside her in a half-turn position, watching her instead of the scenic view in front of them.

Tammy hoped he couldn't see any visible sign of the physical meltdown going on inside her. As it was, she struggled for enough mental strength to engage him in conversation. 'You must have travelled to many places, Fletcher. Is there anywhere more beautiful than this?' she asked, wanting to know more about his life, which was so separate to hers.

'Not like this. Many places have a unique beauty. It's impossible to compare one to the other because they're so different and have an appeal of their own. I prefer more-primitive places than cityscapes. The glaciers in Alaska, Hualong Bay in

Vietnam, the huge herds of wildebeest roaming the Serengeti Plains in Kenya.... Have you ever been outside Australia, Tamalyn?'

She shook her head. 'I've never earned enough money to go.'

'Nursing isn't a well-paid profession,' he said sympathetically. 'Have you graduated to being a fully qualified midwife now?'

'Almost.' She smiled, pleased that he recollected their conversation at Celine's wedding. 'You remembered that about me?'

'Tamalyn of the stormy black hair and violet eyes, the lightning-fast tongue, the natural rhythm of a sensual siren, the heart of an earth-mother... there's nothing I don't remember about you.' He rolled this out as though she was vividly entrenched in his mind.

It was so seductively flattering, Tammy was speechless with surprise and pleasure. It took her several moments to recover her voice and then it was to blurt out, 'I wasn't even nice to you.'

'Nice...' He laughed. 'I get lots of *nice* from women. I prefer spice to nice. Tell me...do you still find the baby business rewarding?'

'Yes. Though it's hard when...' An ungovernable rush of emotion brought tears to her eyes. She'd thought she'd dealt with the tragedy, put it in reasonable perspective, but being with him had somehow undermined the wall of containment she had erected. 'We lost a baby this week,' she said baldly. 'A much-wanted boy. The grief of the parents…' She shook her head as she fought not to completely choke up. 'It was hard.'

'Losing him…it wasn't your fault?'

The concern in his voice, the implied caring for her, squeezed her heart. 'No. There were physical defects. He didn't really have a chance, poor little mite.'

'I'm sure you did all you could for him, Tamalyn.'

'Yes. It's just that sometimes it's not enough, and it hurts that I can't change that because I want to so badly.' She blinked hard to erase the moisture in her eyes, then looked up at him with a wry little smile. 'I don't know why I'm telling you this. It's not what you want from me, is it?'

No fun, she thought. No sharp wit, no spice, totally unsexy. And he was put off by her emotional outpouring, not the slightest gleam of desire left for her in his eyes. They were totally dark, intensely dark, boring into hers as though transfixed by the heart she had just laid bare. When he finally spoke, it was in a strained tone.

'Life and death…you're intimately involved with it on a daily basis, while I—' he grimaced '—I work with numbers, removed from the humanity that touches you all the time.' His hand lifted, featherlight fingers brushing her cheek in a kind of tender salute. 'You shred my pride, Tamalyn.'

'I'm sorry. I didn't mean to carry on. You should have tremendous pride in what you've done, Fletcher. It's so beyond most people's capabilities and…'

His fingers moved to her lips, silencing the anxious rush to give him the importance he deserved.

'I'm the one who should apologise,' he said gruffly. 'Calling what you do "the baby business" was crass. I didn't realise, didn't stop to think there could be pain as well as pleasure in your work. Last time we met, you spoke so happily about becoming a midwife.'

'Mostly it is happy,' she assured him.

'Good!'

He smiled, and it was like sunshine bursting upon her after rain. She hadn't dampened his interest in her, hadn't spoiled anything. He cared about her and it was wonderful to bask in his caring.

'Tell me about your work,' she pressed eagerly, wanting him to share his world with her.

It was so much bigger, very high-level and political, though he was now in an advisory role on the system he and his team had created, passing what he'd called hack work to others. 'My time is more my own. I can choose what I do,' he explained.

Tammy hoped he would choose to spend a lot of it with her.

They stayed on the terrace together, watching the lights come on around the harbour as the twilight darkened, then followed the other guests into the house.

It wasn't a formal reception, more like a cocktail party with drinks and gourmet finger food being regularly circulated. Tammy had never thought of eating being sexy. Somehow Fletcher made it so, watching her mouth when she bit into puff pastry or spooned in the yummy mornay scallops served on shells. He used a drop of sauce falling on her chin to wipe it off with his finger and put it in his own mouth with a slow sensuality that seemed terribly erotic. She found herself licking her lips and it wasn't in appreciation of the fine food. She wanted to taste him, wanted to experience everything about the man he was.

It shocked her how intensely he made her feel. She had no idea if he viewed tonight with her as an end in itself or the start of a relationship he wanted to pursue. She wanted to believe the latter, wanted to believe it had been wrong to close the door on him before, wanted to take whatever he was offering her now.

Despite his sister's and Max Hathaway's presence at the celebration party, he concentrated his interest solely on her. None of her friends interrupted their togetherness and Max Hathaway only briefly intruded on them, pausing to say 'Hello,' and eyeing Tammy with keen curiosity as he remarked to Fletcher, 'I see why you wanted the invite.'

'Thanks for obliging me.'

'You're welcome.'

He nodded to both of them and moved on, without any reference to getting together later or tomorrow or any other time.

So it was true, Tammy thought. Fletcher had come for her. But for how long?

'When do you fly out again?' she asked, needing to know how much time was possible with him.

He grimaced. 'Tomorrow afternoon. I have to be back in Washington this coming week.'

There was only tonight!

'So this is another flying visit to Australia,' she said, trying not to sound desolate with disappointment.

His eyes locked on hers. 'The thought of you drew me here.'

Blatant, burning desire—no attempt to hide it.

'For what, Fletcher?' she blurted out, needing truth from him.

'For whatever we make of it,' he replied.

He was holding out possibilities, no promises. Which was probably fair enough in the circumstances. Yet emotionally, she had an instant recoil against the idea of being a one-night stand which might or might not be extended into a future relationship. Was it a risk she had to take?

'Then I'd better enjoy your dancing expertise while I can,' she said, forcing a challenging little smile. 'If you're up for it.'

It sparked a wicked glitter in his eyes. 'Definitely up with you.'

The DJ was already in action, spinning popular rock music that everyone could jig to. The small dance floor was crowded. There was no room for any showy flair, but room enough for some extremely dirty dancing and Fletcher was every bit as good at that as he'd been with the jazz waltz.

Tammy did not object to the sinfully sensual moves he made. She loved his hands sliding over the curves of her body, loved the feel of the muscular strength in his thighs, and exulted in the hardness of his obvious erection when they rubbed together, grinding rhythmically to the beat of the music.

She felt gloriously, dangerously sexy, every female cell in her body buzzing with feral excitement. This man was her mate. Instinct insisted it was so. Instinct was screaming at her to seize this chance to claim him, to burn herself so deep in his consciousness no other woman could ever reach that place. He would come back to her because he had to.

The music came to a halt and the DJ announced that a few speeches were about to be made. Guests started crowding into the main room to hear them. Waiters were carrying around trays loaded with glasses of champagne. Fletcher grabbed two bubbling drinks, passing one to her as they moved off the dance floor and found a space where they could stand and listen.

Tammy didn't hear a word about the bride and groom. Fletcher positioned himself directly behind her. He played with her hair. He ran a finger down the length of her bared spine. He blew softly on the nape of her neck. He whispered in her ear, 'Can we go after the speeches are done?'

'Go where?' she murmured, acutely sensitive to his touch, the heat emanating from him.

'I have a suite booked in a hotel at Double Bay and a car parked in the grounds behind this house, ready to take us there.'

The low rumble of the words he spoke was like a drumbeat on her heart. A hotel room. A bed for the night. It was a huge moment of decision for her. Yet she couldn't bear to turn away from him now, couldn't bear the thought of losing him.

'I'll have to speak to Kirsty first.'

'Kirsty has four other bridesmaids.' Fletcher reminded her, a terse note of impatience in his voice. 'She doesn't need you to stay on till the end.'

'I won't, but I can't go without saying goodbye.' That was wrong. Maybe going with him was wrong, too. Uncertainty roared through her mind. She swung on him, a harsh bolt of truth shooting out of her mouth, challenging the caring he'd shown her earlier. 'The bond of friendship is worth more than a tumble with you, Fletcher. Kirsty will still be here for me when you're long gone.'

His jaw tightened as though she had slapped him. The light of battle blazed in his eyes, then slowly simmered down to a steady flame of purpose. 'You're not a tumble to me, Tamalyn. I didn't fly halfway around the world for a tumble,' he bit out. 'Perhaps we'll both be able to measure the worth of it tomorrow.'

'Yes,' she said recklessly. 'I'm looking forward to doing precisely that. In the meantime, I won't leave with you until I wish Kirsty every happiness in her marriage.'

The kind of happiness Fletcher might never give her.

She turned her back to him again, frightened of the decision she'd just made, a turbulent whirl of emotional conflict ripping through her as she remembered Celine's warning about her brother—running through women like there was an endless supply of them. Was she any different? Could she hold his interest?

His hands gripped her waist as though needing to claim possession of her. 'Okay. Do what you have to,' he muttered darkly. 'I've waited this long. What's another hour?'

This long... Had she caused him to be disinterested in other women these past six months? Hope soared over her fears. Maybe going with him tonight was not such a mad gamble.

The speeches were followed by the cutting of the cake and a bridal waltz. Tammy had to leave Fletcher to join in the waltz with the groomsman who'd partnered her for the wedding ceremony. As soon as the dance was over, Kirsty announced she was off to the powder room, and Tammy quickly excused herself to go with her.

The only problem was the rest of her friends trouped after them, giving her no chance for a private aside with Kirsty. They crowded into the powder room and verbally pounced on her about Fletcher anyway, so in the face of their observations, there was no point in trying to hide what she intended to do.

'Is it okay with you if I leave the party early, Kirsty?' she asked.

An unholy grin broke out on Kirsty's face as she delivered their old catch-cry. 'Go for it, girl!'

'Yeah...we're all rooting for you,' Lucy chimed in.

'If he's your Mr Right, make him believe you're his,' Jennifer urged.

Hannah gave her a hug and a kiss. 'We just want you to have what *you* want, Tam.'

Celine, who'd repeatedly warned her against any involvement with her brother shook her head in helpless bemusement. 'He obviously came to the wedding for you. I hope it means something good. I'll kill him if it doesn't. You're my friend.'

'Don't worry, Celine. I know what I'm doing,' Tammy quickly assured her—*taking what I can and hoping for more*—then gave Kirsty a hug and a kiss. 'I hope you have a wonderful honeymoon with Paul and a great marriage.'

'Thanks, Tammy. All the best to you, too,' she answered with feeling. 'Now go and make that man love you as much as we do.'

She left to a chorus of well-wishing, returning to the main room to join Fletcher again. Her face was flushed, partly from the embarrassment of having the whole gang aware of her vulnerability to a man who would leave her tomorrow, partly from the rapid pounding of her heart at knowing the moment of decisive action had come.

The old song, 'Tonight,' from *West Side Story* started playing in her mind as she spotted Fletcher across the room and everyone else blurred into non-existence.

There's only you tonight...

The instant her eyes met his, he started moving, making a beeline for her while she stood watching him, waiting, her feet rooted to the floor, her whole being strangely energised by the purposeful force of the man. He was going to take her, sweep her away with him, have what he wanted with her.

Quivers ran through her stomach. A weird weakness invaded her arms and legs. She felt as though her body was surrendering to his will, yet hadn't she made up her own mind about this?

Of course she had.

'Said goodbye to the bride?' he asked, reaching out, taking her hand, squeezing it to affirm the connection with her.

'Yes. It's okay for us to leave now,' she answered, reasserting her own authority over the situation.

He smiled, warm pleasure dancing from his eyes and encompassing everything she was. At least, that was how it felt. 'Then let's go,' was all he said.

His strength seemed to pour into her from their linked hands as they walked out of the house together. The cool night air was revitalising, too, whisking the heat from her face, making her skin tingle with sensitivity. A sudden burst of joy zinged through her. *Tonight...tonight...*sang in her mind again. Her feet wanted to dance, to cavort wildly under the moon and stars, her arms swinging out to the myriad city lights around the harbour as she twirled like a dervish, shedding all the cares of her life, being free.

She laughed at the mad image of herself—

Tammy Haynes, the smart, sensible member of the gang, completely losing her head and going right off the straightline rails she had drawn for the course of her life.

'What's amusing you?' Fletcher asked, his eyes quizzing hers with acute intensity, not liking her being out of his mental loop.

'Me,' she answered, grinning at him. 'I think there must be a pagan streak in me. Any minute now I might howl at the moon.'

He laughed, the taut wary expression relaxing. 'Perhaps there is something to lunar madness.' His mouth curved into a wolfish smile, his eyes glittering with dangerous intent. 'I'm feeling distinctly primitive myself.'

The childhood story of Little Red Riding Hood with the wolf in her grandmother's bed popped straight into her mind. 'Oh my, what big ears you have, Grandmama!' she recited teasingly. 'What big teeth you have!'

'All the better to gobble you up, my dear,' he intoned darkly.

She laughed at his instant response, giddily delighted that he could share her silly mood and exhilaratingly aware that he meant to do just that—gobbling her up in sexual terms—once they reached his hotel room.

Which reminded her there were some things she

had to be sensible about. 'I didn't come prepared for this, Fletcher. I haven't been taking a contraceptive pill or…'

'I'll take care of it. I always use a condom anyway. Though I appreciate the warning, Tamalyn.' He squeezed her hand as he cynically added, 'Some women don't play straight.'

It worried her again—how many women he'd *played* with—if she was just a game to him. Then she firmly told herself there was only one sure way to find out. After tonight she would *know*.

They rounded a high hedge which had hidden the parking lot and she waved at the rows of cars. 'Which chariot is ours?'

'The one with the most horse-power.'

He led her towards a silver Porsche.

'No speeding allowed,' she said with mock gravity.

'In which case…' They'd reached the passenger door and instead of opening it, he swung her into his embrace. '…I need to take a pit stop right now.'

Her heart skipped a beat. 'Hungry, are you?' tripped off her tongue.

'Starving.'

His kiss wiped any further light banter from her mouth, from her mind. If he was starved for her, she was more than starved for him, kissing him back with a reckless abandonment of any inhibitions, flinging her arms around his neck, fingers thrusting into his hair, pressing his head down to hers, demanding the continuation of the fierce flow of passion that was firing from one to the other.

His arms crushed her to him and she revelled in his hunger for all of her, loving the feel of her breasts squashed against the hard hot heave of his chest, the furrowing of her stomach by the strong thrust of his desire for her. She was as feverish as him in wanting and taking every intimacy that could be had.

'Tamalyn, if we don't move now…' Ragged words, bursting with need.

'Yes,' she mindlessly agreed.

He bundled her into the passenger seat, secured her seat-belt, kissed her hard and fast, slammed the door shut, and was around the car to the driver's side and settling himself behind the wheel while she was still catching her breath. The powerful engine roared into life and they were off, headlights scything through the darkness of the park, much brighter than moonbeams, Tammy thought dizzily, a shining path to the bed Fletcher would share with her tonight.

He reached across to her lap, taking strong possession of the hand closest to him, his fingers dragging over her skin, digging in. 'I've never wanted a woman so much,' he said, slinging a smile at her.

It gave her an exhilarating sense of power.

Yet would the wanting last beyond tonight?

She stared down at their linked hands, wishing this togetherness could go on forever. Tonight would not be enough for her. The big critical question was…would it be enough for him?

CHAPTER FIVE

TAMMY was forcibly reminded of Fletcher's billion-dollar status when they arrived at the very exclusive boutique hotel at Double Bay. The silver Porsche should have signposted his wealth but she'd barely noticed it, her mind too occupied by the man who drove it. However, it was impossible to overlook the fact that this hotel was top of the town accommodation, five stars plus, regularly patronised by visiting VIPs. She knew it by reputation but had never been in the place.

Money, money, money…ran through her mind as Fletcher led her into the awesome foyer and she took in the fabulous furnishings and fantastic floral arrangements. Everything oozed classy luxury. Even the elevator doors were made of gleaming brass. Fletcher pressed the button for the top floor. He'd said he'd booked a suite. A penthouse suite?

Not that it mattered. Only the man mattered to her. He had his arm around her, holding her close as they rode up in the elevator. Any minute now they'd be alone together in his suite, privacy guaranteed. A frisson of fear mixed with the buzzing excitement of anticipation, making her nerves tremulous, causing her heart to thump almost painfully. Would she live up to his expectations? Would he live up to hers? So much of who she was seemed to be invested in how this night with him would turn out.

Yet when they entered his suite, she was so stunned by its magnificence, the whirling thoughts in her mind were knocked right out of it. It was all black and white with exotic touches everywhere: white carpet stretching to a wall of windows overlooking the bay and the harbour beyond, black leather lounges with red and gold cushions, a glass table held up by black panthers climbing white rocks, a floral arrangement of red and gold lilies as its centrepiece, black leather chairs around it, and separating the incredibly spacious living space from what she assumed was the bedroom area was a multi-panelled Chinese screen, brilliantly decorated with red-and-gold dragons and mother-of-pearl insets for clouds, trees of jade, wonderfully rich and vivid against the black laquered frames.

'Wow!' spilled from her lips on a long expulsion of breath.

'Like it?' Fletcher asked, shooting her a whimsical little smile.

She rolled her eyes. 'I'm speechless.'

He laughed. 'A first amongst firsts.'

The first time for them. The first time she'd wanted a man so much. The first time she'd ever taken a step without knowing where it would lead her. So many firsts. Did he understand that?

He hugged her more tightly to him, walking her across to the wall of glass, opening a door to the balcony outside. 'Now we can have the harbour completely to ourselves,' he murmured. 'Enjoy the beauty of the night at our leisure.'

It was strange, the rush of pleasure his romantic words evoked. They had been on fire for each other just before the short trip in the car, and she had expected another swift burst of hungry passion from him, had been feverishly anticipating it. Yet it was a sweet relief to feel it wasn't all just sex for him, that there were other things he wanted to share with her besides the strictly physical.

They moved out to the balcony railing, stood side by side, breathing in the night air with its salty tang from the harbour, gazing out at the view that was so unique to this Australian city. 'You're right, Tamalyn,' Fletcher said ruefully. 'There's nowhere else in the world like this. I've never really felt at home in the places I've occupied overseas but I've had to be there for the work, the contacts. One day, when I've finally shed all the responsibilities I'm managing in regard to the project, I'll come back and settle in Sydney.'

With me?

Those two critical words dominated her mind. Impossible to think of anything else to say, and she couldn't say them, couldn't reveal her heart to that extent. She barely knew this man, only knew he affected her as no other did.

Her silence provoked him into turning to her, curling a tendril of her long curly hair around his finger, tugging gently as he asked, 'No comment?'

Best to get her smart tongue working again, she told herself. 'Is that day likely to come anytime soon?'

'No. Too much still to do. But when I heard about Kirsty marrying Max's brother, all I could think of was… Tamalyn…' He rolled out her name as though it was a siren song, an irresistible pull on him. 'I want this night to be ours, something very special between us.'

One night.

Only one night.

Tammy sucked in a deep breath to calm her wildly fluttering heart. Regardless of the strength of the attraction, he'd just warned her he would drop out of her life tomorrow with no promise of ever seeing her again. A dark chill crept through her mind, shrivelling up her hope of love. She'd let herself be fooled by his wanting her so much, he'd flown halfway around the world to be with her. That didn't really mean anything, not for a man of his wealth. He'd simply pursued an urge, determined on having what she'd denied him last time.

She steeled herself to turn and face him, tilting her head inquiringly, injecting a light curiosity into her voice. 'Do you think I'll be less of a distraction to you after tonight?'

He grinned at her flippant tone, probably relieved that she wasn't taking him too seriously. 'I don't know,' he answered, his eyes dancing with seductive devilment. 'I suspect all my nights after this one are going to be haunted by you.'

She hoped so. She savagely hoped so. Because she wasn't going to back out now. Lucy's words rang in her mind—*a climactic moment of pleasure to treasure forever.* At least she might get that from Fletcher Stanton, if nothing else, and she'd know what her friends were talking about when they discussed their sex lives.

'That sounds fair since you won't be here to warm mine,' she tossed at him, pretending a sophistication that hid how gutted she felt.

He laughed and gathered her into his embrace, planting warm little kisses on her temples. 'I love your cut-throat mind, even though it has a habit of setting me back on my heels.'

Love…

Her cut-throat mind went all mushy at the word, no sharp edges left anywhere.

He lifted a hand and gently cupped her face, tilting her chin up so she was forced to meet his gaze. She could only hope her eyes weren't swimming with the deeply treacherous vulnerability he had just tapped. His were too dark for her to read.

'Your eyes are midnight blue,' he murmured. 'You've gone inside yourself, Tamalyn. Tell me what you're thinking.'

'I don't want to talk,' she blurted out. *It hurts and I don't want you to see it hurts.* 'It's not why we're here, is it?'

She couldn't be more cut-throat than that, but it was better for her not to dress this up with romance, better to wipe romance completely off the agenda, because it only muddled her up and she needed to keep a clear head with Fletcher Stanton, not feed futile hopes and dreams.

Take what you can and don't even look for more.

That was the safest thing to do. The sensible thing. A memory to treasure. Because a man like him might not come her way again, and she still wanted to know what it would be like with him.

He frowned. 'You make me feel guilty.'

'Don't be. It's not as if you seduced me.'

The frown deepened, narrowed eyes searching her with probing intensity. 'You're such a special person, Tamalyn. I didn't want you to think I don't value who you are.'

'Then value me in bed. Make it special for me,' she challenged fiercely, tearing herself away from him and heading back inside, hellbent on action.

He didn't follow on her heels. Maybe she'd shocked him out of his socks with her blunt throwing down of the gauntlet between them. Maybe he'd simply paused to put on a condom, ensuring there were no unwelcome consequences from tonight's game.

Whatever…the bottom line was to satisfy the desire they'd been feeling all evening, and he wasn't about to give up on that, not having put so much effort and energy into getting her to this point. She rounded the Chinese screen and stopped dead, staring at the bed. A black silk duvet was draped over white bed-linen.

Black is the colour of my heart, she thought.

Some red and gold cushions were propped against a pile of white pillows.

Red for the bleeding emotional wounds he'd leave her with.

Gold for the value of the memories.

Hands seized her waist and spun her around. 'Too late for cold feet,' Fletcher grated out, his eyes ablaze with a battle light that was not about to be dimmed by anything.

She could see it now—his ruthless intent to win at all costs—and it instantly ignited her own fighting spirit. Be damned if she'd let him go away from this night unscarred!

There was no attempt at seduction in the mouth that crashed down on hers. It plundered. It ravaged. The violent urge to devour all that she was poured from him, to possess with absolute domination, to have nothing escape from him. She held her ground, attacking back with the same all-consuming passion.

He stripped her of her dress. She stripped him of his suit. There was no pause to look at each other. It was all frenzied action, a clash of naked bodies, flesh craving to feel other flesh, hands raking, clutching, kneading, wild kisses fuelling the heat of out-of-control need. He hauled her off her feet for more-intimate connection with him, strode to the bed, her legs dangling against his until she curled them around his thighs, increasing the friction between them, driving up the excitement of imminent total union.

They toppled onto the silk duvet together, almost sliding off it. Fletcher ripped it out from beneath her, hurling it aside, finding more purchase for his knees on the sheets, shifting her up so her head was on the pillows, lifting her hips, plunging himself deep inside her, a raw guttural cry erupting from his throat.

Her body instinctively arched to take in all she could of him, to be absolutely filled by the hot hard length of him, to feel the sensation of encompassing, owning what made him a man—the one man who had stirred this tumult of need in her. There was a moment of sharp pain, but it was instantly followed by an incredibly piercing pleasure, streaking through her entire being as he reached the edge of her womb. Her legs wrapped themselves tightly around his hips to hold him there, but she wasn't strong enough to keep him still. He drove himself in a fast furious rhythm and she rocked with him, realising he was increasing the ecstatic sensation with every thrust forward and not wanting him to stop.

She felt herself teetering on the edge of some unimaginable chaos, her inner muscles convulsing in panic or need—she had no idea which. Her mind had ceased to think. There was only feeling—extremely intense feeling—climbing to a peak she hadn't quite reached. Then there was a sweet sense of gushing as though she was melting inside, and the intensity collapsed into a warm sea of pleasure and she was floating, rolling with the waves of his stroking until he, too, collapsed, as totally spent as she was.

He fell on top of her, breathing hard, and she could feel the racing thump of his heart. Her legs slid away from his, no strength left in them, her whole body suffused by a languor that accepted his weight without any sense of protest. It felt right, good. She wound her arms around him, stroked his back, ran her fingers through his hair, felt a wave of tenderness as though she was soothing a baby. Which was probably quite mad. But then all of this was mad, and so completely beyond any physical experience she'd ever known that it would certainly live in her memory forever.

He raised himself enough to drop a kiss on her forehead, then rolled onto his back, dragging her with him so her body was sprawled over his, her head tucked under his chin. She lay still, luxuriating in the lovely intimate sensation of warm, naked flesh pressed together. He ran his knuckles down the curve of her spine, spread his fingers through her hair, trailing long tresses between them.

She wondered what he thought of what they had just shared, whether it had been in any way extraordinary to him. Had it simply lightened the load of frustration he'd carried or would it live in his memory as something uniquely special?

She couldn't ask. It would sound like a plea for some kind of emotional reassurance which would be out of place in this situation. He'd be gone tomorrow. It was too humiliating to express any need for more than he was giving. Let it be *just sex,* she told herself. If she held on to that attitude, she'd cope much better when he left her.

'Satisfied?'

His voice sounded gruff, almost angry, stirring confusion that she didn't know how to sort through.

'Yes, thank you,' she answered, deciding a simple reply was her best course.

'Why didn't you tell me you were a virgin?' he growled. 'It was too damned late to stop.'

'I didn't want you to stop.'

He heaved himself up so she flopped onto her back and he was leaning over her, bristling with dominating aggression. 'You're twenty-four years old. I didn't expect it. What the hell does this mean, Tamalyn?'

'Like you said…there's a first time for everything. You don't have to make a big deal of it, Fletcher.'

His eyes searched hers with angry intensity. 'Did I hurt you?'

'Only for a second. Everything was quite brilliant after that.'

'Brilliant…' He repeated the word savagely as though he couldn't believe she meant it. 'It wasn't right. It wasn't how I intended it to be. I didn't want Wham! Bam! Thank you, ma'am with you, and be damned if I'll let it go at that.'

She smiled, a fierce satisfaction zinging through her at the realisation she had upset his *winning* plan for tonight. 'I liked it fine the way it was,' she said, wondering if it was possible to drive him off course tomorrow, as well.

He bared his teeth but it wasn't really a smile, more like a dangerous animal about to bite. 'Okay, you've had *your* way. Now we'll have mine. Stay right there!' he commanded, rolling swiftly off the bed, standing over her and holding up a halting hand to forbid any movement. 'I'm going to run a spa bath for us to relax in for a while.'

'Okay.' A bath sounded like a good idea.

Strange, how their physical intimacy had freed her of inhibitions. Here she was, lying in naked abandonment, and actually enjoying watching him walk to a door just beyond his side of the bed, admiring his perfectly male physique: broad muscular shoulders, chest tapering down to lean hips and a taut cheeky butt, strong athletic legs.

He disappeared inside what was obviously an ensuite bathroom. She heard taps running. Then he was back, striding past the Chinese screen to the living area, returning a few minutes later carrying a silver tray loaded with an ice bucket containing a bottle of champagne, two flute glasses and a dish of strawberries with what had to be fancy chocolates wrapped in coloured cellophane.

'I called the hotel and ordered this to be brought up to the suite while you were saying goodbye to Kirsty,' he informed her, eyes flashing determination to pursue *his* plan. 'We shall relax *and* refresh ourselves.'

'How romantic of you!' Tammy mocked, glad she had totally sabotaged his seductive scenario and knocked his arrogant confidence that he could arrange everything his way. 'Do you organise all your one-night stands like this?'

He stopped in his tracks, glaring at her with black resentment. 'No, I don't! I had this ridiculous urge to pleasure you in every conceivable way, Tamalyn Haynes.'

She propped herself up on her elbows, cocking her head consideringly. 'You had a fantasy about me and I spoiled it by not fitting into it as you envisaged. That's why you're vexed.'

His breath hissed out between his teeth. The tension in his face relaxed into an ironic smile. 'I didn't expect the reality to be dynamite, blowing me to smithereens. I need some time to get myself back together. Is it too much to ask for you to oblige me?'

'I like being asked rather than commanded.' And it wouldn't hurt him to start caring about what *she* wanted.

'Right!' The smile gathered some charm. 'Will you join me for a bubble bath?'

'Mmm…some bubbles inside and out should give us a lift,' she said provocatively, casting a wickedly teasing glance below the silver tray with the champagne as she swung herself off the bed. The more she unhinged him from his arrogant confidence, the more he might review her value to him.

'Hope the bathroom provides some pins to do up my hair,' she added, lifting the long tresses from her neck and giving them a tumbling shake while she preceded him into the bathroom, walking with a jaunty sway—actions she hoped were so hypnotically sexy he wouldn't notice any defects in her female physique, like a few cellulite dimples in her bottom.

Her breasts were fine, reasonably full and firm. She had a slender waist, nicely curved hips and good legs. Only her bottom was a bit of a worry and the sooner it was sitting in the spa bath covered by a frothing blanket of bubbles, the more comfortable she'd feel about it.

'You are one hell of a challenging witch. You know that?' came the growled comment behind her.

'Just being me,' she said airily. 'Take it or leave it.'

'Oh, I'll take it,' he drawled, his voice dripping with relish for the task.

Quite clearly her dimpled bottom had not turned him off. Tammy proceeded with more confidence to the vanity bench in the bathroom, intent on searching the drawers for pins. Her hair looked like rats' tails when it was wet, totally unsexy. Having taken Lucy's advice, she was thinking that maybe appealing to the brain below Fletcher's belt might get her to the brain above it.

The bathroom was as splendid as the rest of the penthouse suite—all black marble, gold taps, big fluffy white towels, a very artistic arrangement of red lilies in a sparse Japanese style *and* providing every possible amenity including hair-pins. She eyed her reflection in the mirror as she piled her hair on top of her head in a fairly loose concoction of curls and fastened them in place.

Black hair…a pity she wasn't a witch with the power to keep Fletcher spellbound forever. If she could somehow make this a magic night so he'd keep coming back for more of what they could have together, maybe he would end up loving her, not wanting to live without her, so when he eventually did settle in Sydney…the image of being *his* bride flitted through her mind.

Fantasy…

She smiled wryly at herself. It certainly wasn't his fantasy tonight. Yet if she happily went along with whatever *he* had in mind—providing it was acceptable to her—it was possible this could become a start towards what *she* had in mind.

The champagne cork popped.

The bath was a sea of bubbles. Fletcher turned off the taps and pressed the button to activate the spa. 'It's ready,' he said.

'Great!' She stepped in and settled back against the gently shooting spurts of water, grinning at him. 'Nothing like a spa bath for a feeling of decadence.'

'Let me add to the feeling,' he said, crushing a strawberry into each of the flute glasses, pouring champagne over them, handing her one of the glasses with a very sensual smile. 'A decadent palate cleanser for you.'

She laughed and sipped the delicious drink, her eyes flirting wickedly with his as he joined her in the bath and she stroked her foot up the inside of his thighs. He grabbed it, lifted it out of the water, poured some of his champagne on it and sucked her toes, his dark eyes twinkling wickedness right back as she gasped at the bolt of excitement that shot up her leg.

'I'm going to taste all of you before this night is over.'

'I think I might taste all of you, too,' she quickly retorted, trying not to let him see how deeply he affected her.

He laughed and shook his head. 'You're never going to lie down for me, are you?'

She cocked an eyebrow. 'I thought I already did.'

'Not in your mind, Tamalyn. Not in your mind.'

'Why would I, Fletcher, when you'll be gone tomorrow?'

'You have my full attention right now.'

'And you have mine...right now.'

He gave her a long searing look, searching for a chink in the protective armour she'd pulled around her inner self. She stared back, determined not to surrender her soul to him until he was prepared to surrender his to her.

'Fair enough,' he finally conceded, reaching for a chocolate, removing its cellophane wrap, leaning forward and popping it into her mouth. 'Let's enjoy all there is to enjoy.'

She nodded agreement, biting into the chocolate filled with strawberry cream. She didn't want any pretence from him that this situation was anything other than it was—one night together. The hope that it might lead to more had to be kept hidden. She did have some pride left, enough to cover the truth of how vulnerable she was to being hurt by his departure, not knowing if he would ever return to her.

Enjoying what they could have together tonight was all she could really count on.

So she would enjoy it...every minute of it.

CHAPTER SIX

THE moment of parting was fast approaching. Fletcher had ordered a taxi to take her home and requested the Porsche be brought up from the hotel car-park, ready for him to drive to the airport. His overnight bag was packed, his formal suit zipped up in a carry bag. He was casually dressed in jeans and sweatshirt, ready for his flight to America. Somehow the less formal clothes made him look even more magnetically virile, or maybe the memory of what lay under them was still so fresh in her mind, Tammy couldn't view him without thinking of it.

He was a wonderful lover, surprising and delighting her with so much pleasure, she could not have dreamed how marvellous it had been with him, but it made it even harder to accept that this was all that might be between them. He hadn't said anything about setting up another meeting and she couldn't let herself ask for one.

A painful tension built up in her as she dressed in her bridesmaid's outfit, having nothing else to wear. It would probably look odd for mid-afternoon, but who was to see her apart from some hotel staff and the taxi-driver? It didn't matter. Only holding herself together long enough to give Fletcher a smiling farewell mattered. She couldn't bear him to think she was hurt by his departure. A fierce pride dictated that the situation be handled in a light, carefree manner.

Tears pricked her eyes as she bent to slip on her high-heeled sandals. Desperate for him not to notice any moisture in them, she hurried into the bathroom and attacked the tangled mass of her hair with vigour, wielding the hair-brush hard enough to knock some sense into her head. If she got all emotional, it might make Fletcher feel guilty about stepping so intimately into her life, and guilt would probably wipe out any desire to step into it again. And she wanted him to. Wanted it so much she felt she would die inside if he didn't.

He followed her into the bathroom, smiling at her in the mirror as he took the brush from her hand. 'Let me,' he said, and set about stroking the long tresses with a more gentle, sensual action.

She heaved a sigh to relieve the awful tightness in her chest and managed a smile back at him. 'That's nice.'

His eyes targeted hers in the mirror, probing with frightening intensity. 'So what was it worth to you, Tamalyn?' he asked.

Confusion swirled through the emotional bank she was barely suppressing. It took several moments for her to recollect their conversation at the wedding—her comment about friendship being worth more than a tumble in bed with him and his reply that they would measure the worth of their connection tomorrow.

Her fluttering heart hardened. No way would she reveal her feelings to him without some assurance that he returned them in some measure. 'What was it worth to you?' she countered, her eyes challenging the question in his.

His mouth twitched in wry amusement. 'Still setting me back on my heels. Let me say it was well worth everything it cost me.'

Which probably put her on the same footing as a high-priced prostitute, though he probably wouldn't have flown halfway around the world for one of those, so at least she was on a higher level than that. 'I'm glad you came,' she said, choosing her words carefully. 'I very much enjoyed this time with you.'

'Enough to repeat it at some future date?' he bored in.

A cocktail of joy fizzed through her, 'Yes,' she

said giddily, then sobered enough to quickly add, 'If I'm free.'

He wasn't proposing a serious relationship so she shouldn't let him think she was readily available to him whenever he chose to call. Let him keep chasing her…until he was caught. *If* that was possible.

'I'll need your e-mail address so I can contact you when there's a window of opportunity.'

He wasn't offering his, which meant he didn't want her to chase him. She was right in deciding to maintain a distance. 'Don't expect me to drop everything for you at a moment's notice, Fletcher. Apart from the fact I work shifts at the hospital, which might have to be rearranged to give me the same window of opportunity as you, I might have made other choices by the time you e-mail me.'

He didn't like that last remark. His mouth thinned into a grim line smacking of frustration and angry determination. His eyes narrowed, shading a sharp glitter of speculation. Was he asking himself if she meant it?

Tammy held his gaze, her stomach in painful knots. Had she made too light of what they had shared? Yet her own self-respect demanded that he not view her as his exclusive possession to be taken out and put down at his convenience. He'd given no exclusive commitment to her, only expressing the desire for a repetition of this weekend.

'I'll make it as soon as I can,' he said decisively. 'And give you plenty of notice.'

She smiled, intensely relieved that she'd won such a critical round in the fight for a future with him. 'I'd like that. Thank you.'

There was a wry acknowledgement in his eyes—that taking her compliance with his wishes for granted was not on. Tammy Haynes was her own person, and that wasn't about to change while he spent most of his life overseas.

'It might be a good idea to start taking a contraceptive pill. One can't be too careful,' he advised.

'True,' she agreed. 'I'll take care of it.'

He grinned, as though that was assurance enough of her being available for him. 'I'll make it soon,' he promised.

It wasn't soon enough for Tammy.

Weeks went by with no word from him. It made her wonder if she was taking the contraceptive pill for nothing. She began to hate checking the e-mail inbox on her computer, hated the empty feeling of wretched disappointment it invariably induced, hated having confided to her friends that everything had been fine between her and Fletcher and they'd be seeing each other again.

Kirsty came back from her honeymoon. The gang was due to meet for their monthly luncheon and she hated the inevitable humiliation of having to confess she'd heard nothing from him, hated having to hide the hurt from her friends and weather their sympathy and support. She had been stupid, stupid, stupid to let herself believe there was a chance of a future with him.

The night before the luncheon she once again checked her e-mail inbox, more out of desperation than hope. Incredibly a message from Fletcher popped up. She stared at it in stunned disbelief, almost as if her own angst might have conjured it up, but the words didn't disappear. She read them over and over again, torn by so many conflicting emotions, her whole body ached from the tumult ripping through her.

How does five days on Lord Howe Island appeal to you? November 25–30. Let me know if you can be free and I'll confirm all bookings.

Five days together…two weeks away…notice enough to juggle the time from her job. She'd just passed the final test of her midwifery course so that pressure was behind her. She could manage the short break…but should she?

It was probably just rest and recreation for him—a slice of down time cut from his business schedule. If she went, it would undoubtedly deepen her obsession with him. Yet could she bear not to go, knowing that no other man was ever likely to give her the pleasure that Fletcher did?

Take what you can.

Why not?

Given her own loveless life, didn't that principle still hold true?

So what if the connection was only sexual for him?

She wanted it.

Her fingers tapped out the reply—*Sounds good. Confirm bookings. Let me know when and where to meet you.*

Satisfied there was no hint of desperate yearning in those words, she hit the send command. Five days with him, she argued to herself, was not a lifetime but it was better than nothing.

The gang met at Darling Harbour the next day, having decided on trying one of the restaurants with an outdoors section along the wharf. Kirsty was happily bursting with news about her honeymoon, and Tammy was relaxed enough to enjoy listening to it. Jennifer was also cockahoop about a new man she'd met, declaring he might very well be Mr Right for her. It was not until after they'd eaten their main course that Celine, with an air of taking the bull by the horns, directly questioned Tammy about Fletcher.

'Has my brother been in touch with you?'

'Yes. We're going to Lord Howe Island together for a few days,' she answered off-handedly, not wanting to make a big deal of it in case it didn't turn out well.

The others were delighted to hear he was pursuing the connection, but Celine couldn't stop herself from expressing concern. 'I hope you're not hanging your heart on him, Tammy. I realise he can give you a good time with all his money, but he's such a self-contained beast—' she shook her head '—I just don't see him as husband material.'

'You're his sister,' Lucy pointed out in exasperation. 'Don't be such a spoilsport, Celine. Besides, Tam is smart enough to work things out for herself. I think a few days alone together on Lord Howe would sort things out fairly quickly. Make-or-break time.'

'Good point!' Hannah chimed in. 'And Tam could do with a lovely break. She's been so serious, working her head off all year to become a midwife…'

'Oh, lord, I've been so full of myself I forgot!' Kirsty broke in. 'Did you pass the final test, Tam?'

'Yes.'

'Great! Let's have a bottle of champagne with our sweets to celebrate.'

'Celebration is definitely in order!' Jennifer declared. 'It's been a big year. Two weddings, one fully qualified midwife…' She raised her eyebrows at Celine and Kirsty. 'Any babies on the way yet?'

'No!' they chorussed.

Everyone relaxed into laughter and there were no more awkward moments for Tammy. Privately she took comfort from what Lucy had said. Five days was a long time to be more or less alone together. Would the attraction fizzle out with so much proximity, or cement itself as something deeply solid? The only way to know was to go, and it was best that she did.

After she'd parted from her friends, she went home and looked up Lord Howe Island on the Internet, wanting to know why Fletcher had chosen it and what clothes she should take to fit in with the island's attractions. She knew there was a yacht race from Sydney to Lord Howe every year, knew the island lay off the far north coast of New South Wales, but that was the sum of her knowledge.

The information on the computer was intriguing. Apparently, the island was an environmental paradise, World Heritage listed for its outstanding beauty and its exceptional biodiversity, two thirds of it a permanent park preserve and its surrounding waters a marine park. It was one of the cleanest places on earth, no air or sea pollution and no litter. It was six hundred kilometres east of the Australian mainland and—an interesting point—beyond the reach of mobile phone calls.

There was no big holiday resort hotel, very few shops and a number of fine restaurants in different locations. Only four hundred visitors were permitted at any one time, and accommodation was distributed amongst seventeen properties which were mostly family operated. The activities listed were bushwalking, trekking, bicycling, swimming, surfing, scuba diving, snorkelling, kayaking, bird-watching, deep-sea, rock and shore fishing, picnics, golf, tennis, bowls.

This was not some exclusive playground for the rich and famous, more a place to totally unwind and get back to nature, a place where one could breathe fresh air, relax and revitalise. It reminded Tammy that Fletcher had said he liked primitive places, preferring views of nature to cityscapes. This island wasn't exactly primitive but it certainly wasn't spoiled by civilisation.

Had he chosen it because it was what he liked and wanted to know if she would enjoy it, as well—a place to share or a place to divide? If he was jaded by a heap of gold-digging women wanting to dig their claws into him, as Celine had implied, maybe this was a test of whether she was attracted to the man or the money—no luxury pent-house suite this time around.

Hope swelled anew.

Five days did suggest serious feelings for her.

The two weeks sped by. Fletcher e-mailed her with more details about their trip. Their flight to Lord Howe was scheduled for 9:00 a.m. on the twenty-sixth. Since he'd be flying in from Los

Angeles earlier that morning, he would meet her in the departure lounge. All she had to do was get herself and her luggage to the domestic terminal at Mascot, pick up her boarding pass at the check-in counter, and he'd be waiting for her.

She had a shopping frenzy, indulging herself with some very sexy lingerie and buying a stack of new casual clothes, mix-and-match sets so she could keep her packing light—only fourteen kilograms of checked baggage was allowed on flights to Lord Howe. The walking shoes were heavy so she decided to wear them, along with her new blue jeans, an orange singlet top, and the cute denim jacket with its floral pattern in tones of blue and cream and orange and dark red. She needed the confidence of looking good—of feeling bright and beautiful—when Fletcher laid eyes on her again.

He'd only ever seen her at weddings.

And the one morning after.

Dressed to the nines or naked, nothing in between.

When she left her apartment to catch the train to the airport on the designated day, her excitement over their imminent meeting was tempered by a rush of nervous fear that she wouldn't live up to his expectations—or he wouldn't live up to hers. This situation was completely different to their previous encounters. It brought on such an anxious state of mind, she found herself double-checking everything: the contents of her wallet, the train connections that had to be made, the time ticking by.

She arrived at the domestic terminal without any problem cropping up. At the check-in counter, all she had to do was identify herself and she was handed a boarding pass with the instruction to proceed to the departure lounge for Gate 24. It was a long walk through the terminal, past the airport shops, past the vast food hall, down a corridor lined with other departure lounges. She counted them off—sixteen, eighteen, twenty, twenty-two— trying to ignore the fact that her legs were getting more jelly-like with every step and her heart was thumping in her ears.

Twenty-four…

Her feet stopped dead when she spotted him. He sat in the middle of a row of chairs, reading a newspaper, his strikingly handsome face wearing an air of tired concentration. Travel weary, she thought, and marking time until he had to move again. It made her wonder how many airports he had waited in over the years and whether he'd truly be content to settle in Sydney once all the project business was done and travelling was no longer necessary.

He looked up and caught her watching him. The fatigue instantly dropped from his face. His eyes lit with pleasure. He dazzled her with a brilliant smile as he rose to his feet, folding the newspaper, discarding it on the chair. Then he was walking towards her, bringing to life again how tall and dynamically attractive he was. He wore black jeans and a black-and-white shirt, black Reeboks on his feet—anonymous kind of clothing but they didn't make Fletcher look anonymous. They seemed to emphasise the innate force of the man.

Tammy didn't think of moving herself. She was too focussed on taking in everything about him, feeling the strength of his drawing power on her, the acceleration of her pulse, the ache of yearning in her belly.

'Don't I rate a greeting?' he asked, whimsically challenging her silence.

'Just checking that you match my memory of you,' she retorted, smiling to reassure him on that score. 'It has been a while and this little jaunt to Lord Howe Island could have been a big mistake.'

His eyes twinkled wickedly. 'I'm glad you took the risk.'

'I'm glad you thought of me.'

'I wanted a release from thinking of you, Tamalyn. Being with you is much more to my liking.'

'I thought you were going to say much more to your taste,' she said provocatively, fluttering her eyelashes as she dropped her gaze to his mouth. 'Would a kiss be a rate-worthy greeting?'

He flashed his wolfish grin. 'Let me rate it.'

She stepped forward, feeling positively petite next to him without the benefit of high heels. Nevertheless, it was a lovely sensual pleasure to slide her hands up his chest and around his neck as she raised herself on tip-toe. He didn't wait for her to pull his head down to meet hers. His arms swiftly enclosed her in an embrace that almost lifted her right off her feet. Nor did he wait for her to initiate the kiss.

It was like he was claiming possession of her again, his mouth taking hers on the same intensely passionate journey they'd shared before—a kiss that searched and found the response he wanted, then revelled in the fierce desire coursing through both of them, the need to recapture and hold on to the explosion of feeling that made time and place irrelevant.

'Is there a broom closet somewhere close?' he muttered when his mouth finally broke from hers.

Laughter bubbled from her throat at how rawly desperate he sounded. She tilted her head back, her eyes teasing his urgent need even as she exulted in it. 'I didn't see one. Besides, that was supposed to be a greeting, not an incitement to find a broom closet at an airport. We do have five days of privacy ahead of us.'

His mouth twitched into an ironic smile. 'It's the thunderbolt effect. I forgot it was a greeting.'

'Which you were supposed to rate,' she archly reminded him.

'Worth every minute I've waited,' he rolled out with feeling.

She laughed again, joy rippling through her. It was great to be with him again. And she had five wonderful days more of him ahead of her. It felt so right. It had to turn out right.

CHAPTER SEVEN

THE flight to Lord Howe was less than two hours, and Fletcher spent the whole time drawing Tammy out about her life since they had last been together, fending off any questions about his own. She obliged him by prattling on about her work at the hospital, passing the final test that meant she would graduate as a midwife, the monthly luncheon with the gang of six.

'You've never mentioned family to me, Tamalyn,' he commented at one point, eyeing her curiously. 'Don't you have one?'

She winced. It was not a subject she liked talking about and tried to brush it off quickly. 'Not really. I'm an only child. I guess you could say I've made my friends my family.'

'Yes, you've made it clear they're important to you, but what of your parents? You're not close to them?'

'It's hard to be close to someone who isn't there for you,' she stated bluntly.

He frowned. 'What do you mean?'

Realising he was going to keep pressing her on the subject, she rattled out some bald facts. 'My parents were divorced when I was very young. I was excess baggage that neither my mother nor father wanted in their desire to move on. A string of nannies looked after me until I was deemed old enough to take care of myself. At eighteen I was presented with a small car and a studio apartment at North Sydney. I've lived an independent life ever since. Enough said?'

'A lonely life,' he remarked.

'It would have been without my friends.'

'My mother and Celine are very close. I would have thought most mothers and daughters are. What's the problem with yours, Tamalyn?'

She shook her head. If her mother met Fletcher and knew he was worth billions, not even the fact that he was twenty years younger would stop her from trying to ensnare him to the point where she could get a big chunk of that money out of him. Telling him how it was with her mother might start him wondering if the daughter was cut from the same mould. Tammy didn't want to put a gold-digging question mark in his mind.

'I'd rather talk about something more cheerful.' She seized on a bit of news she hadn't told him, smiling brightly as she delivered it. 'Jennifer thinks she's found her Mr Right so maybe there'll be another wedding soon.'

His mouth curled sardonically. 'Who's the lucky man?'

His expression of cynical disinterest instantly reminded her of their divisive conversation at Celine's wedding when he had arrogantly scorned her friends for viewing marriage as their ultimate ambition. It hadn't been a fair comment to her mind then, and she didn't like his tone now. Any couple finding they were right for each other *were* lucky.

'He's an author,' she answered, refusing to let him diminish her pleasure in her friend's happy excitement. 'Jennifer works in PR for a publishing company and she took this guy—his name is Adam Pierce—on a publicity tour and they hit it off straight away.'

'Adam Pierce...' Fletcher mused over the name. 'There was an article about him in this morning's newspaper—an overnight sensation, his first book on the *New York Times* bestseller list.'

To Tammy's relief, the cynicism in his eyes was replaced with genuine interest.

'That's him,' she confirmed. 'He wrote an erotic thriller, and it's taken off in a big way. Jennifer gave me a free copy and I've brought it with me to read on the island.'

Fletcher grinned at her, his dark eyes dancing

wickedly as he reached over and took her hand, his fingers threading evocatively between hers. 'You can share the erotic bits with me.'

Heat coursed up her arm and spread through her entire body. Her mind lost all reasoning power, flooded with memories of how wonderfully erotic Fletcher had made the sex between them last time. The desire to feel everything with him again attacked her so strongly she almost squirmed in her seat. Fortunately, the steward announced they were coming in to land, and since Tammy had the window seat, she quickly turned her gaze to get an aerial view of the island, needing some distraction from the wild feelings Fletcher evoked.

It was in the shape of a crescent, the remains of an extinct volcano. There were rocky cliffs at one end, two mountains with their tops wraithed in clouds at the other, and a very green plateau in between with beaches on either side edging lagoons of gorgeous turquoise water. The outer reefs were outlined by the incoming surf breaking against them into masses of white froth. There were no obvious signs of habitation. The island had a primaeval look about it, a piece of exotic nature planted in the middle of pristine blue ocean.

'It's beautiful,' she murmured.

'Yes. And completely unspoiled,' Fletcher said with satisfaction.

'You've been here before?' She turned her gaze back to him, wanting him to elaborate on his reasons for this choice.

His mouth curved in a reminiscent smile. 'About twenty years ago. A school vacation with my parents and Celine. Best vacation I ever had.'

'So you're returning to a memory. Twenty years is a long time. It might have changed since then.'

'No.' His eyes were serenely certain. 'That's the beauty of Lord Howe. It's like a national treasure, valued for what it is.' He squeezed her hand. 'You'll see. I wanted you to share my pleasure in it.'

Her heart leapt with joy. Apart from physical intimacy, he'd shared so little with her. This island was clearly special to him and he'd chosen to bring *her* here. Surely that meant she was special to him, too. It wasn't just about sex. Tammy hugged this lovely warm thought to herself as the plane landed. Five days with Fletcher were bound to reveal more of the inner man—not so much his super-brain but his heart and soul.

Hope was a hopelessly uncontrollable thing.

It simply would not lie down and die.

They alighted from the plane and walked across the runway to a white picket fence that enclosed a beautifully mown green lawn with park benches for people to sit on while waiting for flights, and a house that was apparently the airport terminal.

Cows grazed in a pasture beyond the runway. Tammy couldn't help smiling at how quaintly old-world and low-key it all was, almost as though they were stepping back in time to a different era when life was very simple.

They were met by the owner of their accommodation, who took charge of their luggage and ushered them to a minivan. As he drove them along the island road, which ran between towering Norfolk pines and masses of palm trees, he pointed out the bowling club, the school, the hospital, the island museum, the bicycle hire shop, the boat-shed where they could arrange snorkelling and diving trips or go out to the reef in a glass-bottom boat. All these places were well spaced out along the road, and they passed no cars, only people walking or riding bikes, which was the most common form of transport on the island.

They turned a corner to what their driver jokingly called the main business district. It comprised the community hall, a place called the co-op shop where the islanders brought and sold their local produce, a general store, a beauty salon, a clothing shop, and a café/restaurant called Humpty Dick's where—they were advised—they could buy themselves a nice lunch. Or breakfast. Or dinner. Whatever they liked.

Tammy grinned at the name. Someone had a

very sexual sense of humour. Fletcher squeezed her hand, having taken possession of it again once they were settled in the van. His grin shared her amusement, and the highly sensual pressure of his touch heightened her awareness of how soon they would be sharing so much more…alone together.

The rest of the instructions being given floated around a buzzing core of anticipation in her mind. It was impossible to give her full attention to them, but she listened, not wanting Fletcher to know how dominant her yearning for him was.

They could also get breakfast and lunch at the museum café and dinner at other restaurants which they'd find listed in their apartment. If they booked into a restaurant for an evening meal they would be picked up and brought home so they didn't get lost in the dark. Alternatively they could buy provisions from the co-op, the general store, the top shop, which was closest to their apartment, or Joy's shop, which was near the museum, and cook for themselves in their own kitchen.

All this information brought home how far this island was from being a high-rise tourist resort bustling with holiday-makers. Even the various accommodation places they passed were virtually hidden away behind palm trees and shrubbery. When they finally arrived at the property where Fletcher had booked them in—the closest one to

Ned's Beach which was the most popular beach on the island they were told, it too was secluded behind trees and beautifully nestled in tropical gardens, offering an immediate sense of exclusive tranquillity.

Peace and privacy, Tammy thought. No one would bother Fletcher here, even if they'd read the publicity about him and recognised his name. It made her doubly aware of how intimate these five days were going to be—definitely a test of how *right* they were for each other on a very basic level. As Fletcher helped her out of the van, the simmering look in his eyes set her nerves twitching at how basic he intended it to be as soon as they were left in total privacy.

The colonial architecture of the low-level buildings was charming, reinforcing the idea of a bygone era—tin roofs with bullnosed eaves, verandahs with wooden railings, inviting time to sit out and simply enjoy the ambience of the island. Inside their apartment the decor was tropical with cane furniture and fabrics printed with hibiscus flowers. Every modern convenience was supplied in the kitchen and bathroom. They were given a rundown on how everything worked and told that the licensed restaurant in the main house was open for dinner.

Having thanked their driver/guide, Fletcher ushered him out and closed the door on the outside world. Tammy took a deep breath. This was it—the real beginning of what this time with Fletcher was about. Her pulse was racing, her heart thundering in her ears. Her gaze was fixed expectantly on him as he turned from the door, a wide grin on his face, his dark brilliant eyes sparkling with devilment.

'Happy with where we are?'

'Yes,' she answered huskily, her throat dry from the heat burning through her.

He laughed as he walked to where she stood in the middle of the living room. 'I could have flown you to the most expensive resort on this planet, fitted you out with glamorous clothes, pampered you with every luxury, had the red carpet rolled out for us everywhere we went. I've been totally selfish in choosing this place, wanting you to myself.' He drew her into his embrace, his eyes suddenly serious, keenly probing hers. 'Sure you're not disappointed?'

'I came for you.' It was the simple truth. She slid her arms up around his neck, inviting what she wanted. 'And I'm on the pill now, so why don't you just give yourself to me, Fletcher?'

He smiled. 'That was worth waiting for, too. I didn't want to think about condoms with you.'

'Was that why *soon* wasn't so soon?' She wasn't sure she liked that kind of calculation, waiting for the pill to be absolutely safe.

'Tamalyn, normally I wouldn't trust any woman.

You, I do. Let's leave it at that. We're here…in *this* moment. No more waiting.'

Trust…it was a sweet word. It meant a lot to Tammy, making her even happier that she was here with him.

They kissed in a frenzy of hunger for each other, hands eagerly, urgently re-learning each other's bodies as clothes were hastily discarded, Fletcher sweeping her up in his arms and carrying her into the bedroom, both of them too excited, too needy to wait a moment longer for the intense satisfaction of the ultimate intimacy.

It was sex at its most basic, a wild, primitive drive to possess and be possessed, exulting in the sense of mutual passion for total fusion, the wild incitement to give and take and rise together to the exquisite tension before climax, feel it coming, feel it burst upon them, hug the sheer ecstacy of it, then slowly, slowly slide into euphoric contentment, lying nestled together, snug in their private little world, stripped naked of everything but themselves.

'Tamalyn…'

Her back was turned to him but she heard the smile in his voice as he said her name.

'What?' she asked, wriggling around to face him, a smile on her own face.

His eyes were soft, warm with pleasure. 'Nothing. Just good to be with you again.'

'Mmm…' It was a hum of agreement. 'I'd have to say I'm definitely not disappointed.'

Nor was she disappointed in anything they did on the island over the next five days. The book Jennifer had given her was never opened. Being with Fletcher made every activity exhilarating from the challenge of the guided climb to the summit of Mount Gower, to feeding the huge kingfish that swarmed into the shallows at Ned's Beach.

On other walks she marvelled at the massively spreading groves of banyan trees—weirdly exotic towering over all the palms—and loved the boat trips that took them on snorkel tours of the best viewing areas around the coral reef. Even the food tasted better—the home-baked cakes, freshly caught seafood, locally grown tomatoes. Everything about Lord Howe was marvellous, and sharing the pleasure of it with Fletcher made it absolutely magical.

The sexual attraction between them was so constant and vibrant, just a touch of the hand, a smile, a flash of eye contact, and her body was happily humming in anticipation of the next opportunity for intimacy. She fell so madly in love with him she stopped thinking of it as sex.

They made love.

On the beach.

On top of a cliff underneath a lone Norfolk pine.

On the pontoon in the middle of the lagoon.

Every night, the moment they returned to the apartment after dining out.

Every morning before setting off to Humpty Dick's for breakfast.

Many times Tammy thought it was like a honeymoon in a private paradise. It couldn't have been any better for Kirsty and Paul than this. Except Kirsty and Paul were married and had the emotional security of knowing they would have each other for the rest of their lives.

Fletcher never mentioned the future. Nor did he ever speak the word *love*. Tammy tried to keep a mental door shut on these concerns, determined not to bring any pain into the pleasure of having what he *was* giving of himself. Besides, this time together was so good, she told herself he would surely want to continue their relationship. It was just a matter of waiting until he did bring it up, probably just before they left the island.

They lazed the last morning away, basking in the sun at Ned's Beach, going for the occasional swim to cool off. Fletcher said nothing about meeting up again. Tammy tried to remain relaxed but she could feel the tension of uncertainty building up in her on the walk back to their apartment. Their flight left at one-thirty. They'd only left themselves time to have a quick lunch and do last-minute packing before they'd be collected for the drive to the airport. Was Fletcher content to leave this as simply a shared time out from their different lives?

They passed the island cemetery. On a previous walk they'd strolled along the neat rows of headstones, reading them and speculating about the lives and deaths of beloved wives, husbands and children—island families with long histories here. She desperately wanted much more of a history with Fletcher than a haphazard series of encounters fitted in between long absences.

His silence caused her to withdraw inside herself. Even the hand holding hers lost its power to keep her deeply connected to him. She had to achieve enough emotional detachment to make the inevitable parting with some dignity, no begging, no breaking into tears, a nonchalant acceptance of ships passing in the night. *Again!*

'I can feel you separating yourself from me, Tamalyn.'

His sensitivity startled her into blurting out what to her was a cruel truth. 'Well, it's not as if I can hang on to you, is it, Fletcher?' She shot a wry glance at him, needing some reassurance of some lasting attachment to her but not expecting it. 'Time's almost up and you'll be back on the other side of the world tomorrow.'

He'd already told her his return flight to Los

Angeles was scheduled two hours after they landed back in Sydney and he'd be moving straight from the domestic terminal to the international one.

'I should thank you for sharing this with me,' she rattled on, trying to sound bright and cheerful. 'It's been great!'

'Yes, it has,' he agreed. 'I'm glad you were free.'

'That's it?'

The sharp words were out before pride could stop them, and once said she couldn't take them back. Besides, she was sick of all her inner angst. She *needed* to know. Her heart pounded with apprehension. The heat of many turbulent emotions flared into her cheeks as her feet halted and she swung to face him, her eyes sharply probing his, searching frantically for what she meant to him.

'That's it, Fletcher?' she repeated, her chin jutting with determination not to back down from an open confrontation.

For a moment his eyes blazed with triumphant satisfaction, making her heart pound even faster because she didn't understand what it meant and it frightened her.

'Not if you don't want it to be,' he said with an air of ruthless challenge.

She shook her head in confusion. 'Haven't I just made it clear that I don't want what we've shared here to end?'

'It doesn't have to end.' He stepped closer, raised a hand, ran his knuckles softly down her cheek. 'You can be with me, Tamalyn. The demands of my work keep me overseas, and I find a long-distance relationship both inconvenient and frustrating. I want you with me every day, every night. All you have to do is say yes to that and I'll make all the arrangements.'

Tammy's heart cramped as the realisation hit her that he'd trapped her into revealing too much of it. He'd been waiting for some vulnerability to play on, to take advantage of, to use in gaining his own end. Her chest was so tight with shock she could barely find breath enough to speak.

'You're asking me to leave my life in Sydney to be with you, wherever you are?' she choked out.

'What do you lose?' he asked with arrogant confidence. 'You're now a fully qualified midwife. You can use that anywhere or come back to it at a later time. You're not going to upset a family that cares about what you choose to do with your life. If you want to fly back for the monthly luncheon with your friends, or fly them to you, I'm happy to pay whatever it costs to keep you happy. I can buy you anything you want, Tamalyn.'

'No…no, you can't.' Her feet started stumbling backwards, away from his touch, his reach. She shook her head vehemently over his claim. 'You can't buy my self-respect, Fletcher.'

'What the hell does that mean?'

'It means I won't be a rich man's mistress, giving up my life for his convenience.'

He stepped forward, grabbing her upper arms to halt her retreat from him, fingers digging into her flesh with almost bruising strength, his eyes blazing a command for her to fall in with his plan. 'I'm asking you to be my partner, not my mistress.'

'No, you're not. Partners do equal sharing, and there's nothing equal about this. It's all your way, Fletcher. You just want to have me handy for as long as you find me desirable, and you'll keep me in luxury for as long as I please you.' She'd seen it enough times with her mother to know how it worked and how it ended. 'That's not being partners. It's a barter thing and I won't enter into it.'

His jaw clenched in fighting mode. 'You didn't mind me paying for these past few days,' he bit out.

'I didn't realise you thought you were buying me,' Tammy shot back at him in sharp resentment at having her acceptance judged so cynically. 'I thought I was your guest. But if you see it now as a financial loss, please send me an account for half the cost and I'll pay it.'

'It's irrelevant!' he snapped.

'Not to me, it isn't!'

They glared at each other for long fraught

moments, her fierce pride fighting his equally fierce will to have his way.

'You don't want this to end here any more than I do,' he stated with vehement conviction.

'I didn't understand what "this" was to you, Fletcher.'

'What were you hoping for...a proposal of marriage?' His eyes savagely mocked any such ambition on her part.

I was hoping you would come to love me, to love me so much you'd want me with you always.

Impossible to say such words in the face of his mockery.

Her silence goaded him into a further strike at her heart.

'Did you think giving me your virginity would persuade me to consider making you my bride?'

'I just told you I wasn't into bartering, Fletcher,' she threw at him, her own eyes stormy with rejection of everything he was suggesting. 'Please take your hands off me and let me go back to our accommodation. I have some last-minute packing to do.'

He lifted his hands away in a dismissive flourish. 'Fine! We'll both do that.'

They walked on together but apart, each wrapped in their own tense brooding silence.

Tammy was so churned up inside, as soon as they reached their apartment, she locked herself in the bathroom and was violently ill. She stayed there for as long as she reasonably could, taking a long shower, packing her toiletries, then vacating it for Fletcher to clean up while she dressed in her travel clothes, completed her packing and checked the rooms for anything missed. Her stomach revolted at the thought of eating anything. She tidied the kitchen, took her bag out to the front verandah and sat there waiting for their lift to the airport.

Fletcher did not speak to her, and Tammy did not speak to him.

On their way to catch their flight back to Sydney, he sat beside the driver of the minibus, chatting away to him as though nothing of any importance had happened. Tammy sat behind them, staring out the window, the island paradise now just an empty blur.

Fletcher handled the formalities at the airport terminal. Tammy hung back a little, with him but not beside him. As soon as her bag was checked in and he'd collected their boarding passes, she moved out to the front lawn, settling on a bench seat to wait for the plane to come in. She fixed her gaze on the cows grazing in the paddock beyond the tarmac and emptied her mind of everything to do with Fletcher Stanton.

He came and sat beside her. She ignored his presence, but the tension of doing so made her feel sick again.

'If you think you can bring me to heel, you're making a big mistake, Tamalyn,' he advised her in a derisive tone. 'I won't make another offer.'

She dragged her gaze off the cows to face him with her truth. 'It isn't the life for me. Let's leave it at that.'

There was a flash of angry incredulity in his eyes. Tammy turned away from it. He didn't love her. He hated losing, wasn't used to being refused by a woman. She'd left no room for argument and he disdained attempting to persuade her into a change of mind.

Their plane arrived. The incoming passengers disembarked. They boarded. She and Fletcher were seated together but they couldn't have been more apart. Tammy closed her eyes, concentrating on trying to control the nausea rolling around in her stomach. It was an enormous relief to her when they finally landed at Mascot. Fletcher had only brought a carry-on bag. They could separate as soon as they were inside the terminal.

She expected him to walk off without another word, but he didn't. They were heading down the long corridor towards the exit and the baggage carousel hall when he grabbed her arm to halt her. It jolted Tammy into looking at him, although her eyes were glazed with the urgent need to go to the ladies' room, which they'd almost reached.

'Think about it!' he commanded, his eyes blazing frustration at her stubborn refusal to weaken and give in to what *he* wanted. 'You have my e-mail address. All you have to do is send a *yes*.'

She dragged her arm out of his hold, shaking her head at this last-minute attempt to change her decision. 'It will always be no. Goodbye, Fletcher.'

She spun away from him and dived into the ladies' room.

He was gone when she emerged from it.

The break was complete.

CHAPTER EIGHT

The Third Wedding

THE baby wedding, the gang was calling it. Celine was expecting her first and Lucy was pregnant, too, which was why she was getting married in a hurry.

'It's not a shotgun wedding,' she had insisted. 'Tony and I love each other to bits. We just couldn't keep our hands off each other and…well, never mind about that. Tony's thrilled about becoming a father, can't get it legal fast enough, and his family wants to put on the wedding at their vineyard in the Hunter Valley, so we don't have to worry about finding a decent reception place in Sydney at such short notice.'

Tammy was happy for Lucy and didn't want to steal her thunder by revealing her own pregnancy. She was still coming to terms with it herself. Even when the signs had been piling up, pointing to the fact, she had recoiled from believing it. Not once had she missed taking the pill, continuing to follow the whole month's program after she'd returned from Lord Howe Island. At first, she'd told herself that giving it up after two months of taking it had messed up her menstrual cycle. But the prickling tightness in her breasts, the queaziness in the mornings…she'd had to face up to it.

The pregnancy test had been chillingly positive. No joy in it for Tammy. Fletcher would certainly not be thrilled to learn he was going to be a father. He'd trusted her to take care of contraception. He'd probably think she'd deliberately tricked him, trying to force him into a wedding he didn't want. All she could think of was her system must have rejected the effect of the pill on that last day when she'd vomited her heart out.

Becoming a single mother would not have been her choice, not for herself nor the child, but terminating the pregnancy was not an option she could consider. She loved babies and would love her own, all the more because she couldn't imagine having anyone else to love. Sometime after Lucy's wedding, she would tell her friends, knowing they would be caring and supportive once they'd vented their feelings on what she should do about Fletcher.

To her mind, there was nothing to be done.

In the four months since they had parted at Mascot Airport, he had not contacted her and she had not contacted him. She'd told the gang that her time with him on Lord Howe Island had proved to her they had no future together. End of story. Book closed. Re-opening it was going to be hard and it could certainly wait until after Lucy's wedding.

Although the Hunter Valley was only three hours' drive north of Sydney, Tammy had never visited the famous wine region, hadn't realised it was such a tourist industry. The Andretti Vineyard was a stunning eye-opener for her. Not only were there seemingly endless rows of grapevines stretching off into the distance, but there was a thriving business attached to it; a large restaurant with an open-air courtyard surrounded by a beautiful rose garden, an arts and craft shop selling the work of local artists, an amazing underground cellar for wine-tasting, the huge sheds where the wine was made and bottled, and a motel where she and her friends and other wedding guests were being accommodated during the weekend.

She did know that the Fine Wines Emporium Tony managed in Sydney was owned by his family. She simply hadn't envisaged the extent of the business behind it. This was a wonderful place for a wedding, much more interesting than a function room in the city. And the weather was kind—a lovely fine day for the ceremony under the courtyard pergola which was covered with climbing roses.

Adjoining motel suites were being used by the

six of them to get dressed, help each other look their best and share the excitement of the build-up to Lucy's big moment. They were all wearing empire style dresses, mirroring the style of Lucy's bridal gown, which was designed to hide her slightly rounded tummy.

The gown was beautiful, its V-necked bodice appliqued with lace and a band of pearls underneath the bustline. There were rows of lace flowers around the long flowing skirt and cascades of pearls hanging from them near the hem.

Purple satin had been chosen for the bridesmaids and matrons of honour because it suited the vineyard, with its dark grapes that made the famous Andretti red wine. They were halter-necked dresses with a gathering of fabric fastened under the bust by a silver sunburst broach, the skirt falling in graceful folds from this centrepoint. Tammy was grateful that it skimmed her figure rather than hugged it. Although she had no baby bulge as yet, her waistline had thickened and she hadn't wanted that to be obvious to anyone.

The colour looked great on her and she loved the high-heeled silver sandals they'd all bought together, loved the silver necklace and earrings Tony had presented them with. Her long hair had been done up in a high sophisticated top-knot, with a couple of curled tendrils hanging down in front of her ears. She was looking good and feeling good, all primed to thoroughly enjoy Lucy's wedding until...

'Is that a helicopter coming in?' Kirsty asked, frowning over the intrusive blast of increasing noise overhead.

'No doubt it's Fletcher doing his last-minute-arrival thing,' Celine said with a roll of her eyes. 'Who else would turn up in a helicopter?'

Fletcher!

Tammy felt as though she'd been hit by a brick.

'Why would he be coming to *this* wedding?' she blurted out in shocked protest.

It turned all eyes to her. Embarrassed heat spurted into her cheeks. 'Why didn't anyone tell me?' she demanded, hurt by what felt like a conspiracy of silence.

'You said it was over, Tam,' Jennifer quietly reminded her. 'What difference does it make?'

'My parents have always been close friends with Celine's. Naturally they put Fletcher on the guest list,' Lucy explained. 'Since the two of you broke up I didn't actually expect him to come. When he accepted the invitation, it made me think... well, maybe he wants another chance with you, Tam, and you've looked so peaky since whatever the blow-up was about on Lord Howe—' she spread her hands in apologetic appeal '—I thought it might be good for you to meet up again.'

Tammy fought for control. Her chest was so tight she was struggling not to hyper-ventilate. Lucy meant well. She always meant well. It was just that her past advice had not proven good and her current meddling…no, it wasn't really meddling…

Kirsty wrapped an arm around her shoulders and gave them a warm squeeze. 'We all thought it, Tam. Thought he might have learnt from his mistakes and you'd be happy to revisit what you meant to each other. You were in so deep with him…'

Tammy could feel the blood draining from her face. Her friends had no idea how deep. She was having his child and he'd probably hate her for it.

'We weren't sure he would actually come in the end and we didn't want to raise hopes,' Hannah rushed in anxiously. 'But if you don't want any contact with him, you can stick with the wedding party, Tam. We'll look after you.'

She would have to tell him about her pregnancy. It was impossible to postpone such a critical piece of news in a face-to-face situation.

'What did my brother do to you?' Celine shot out, looking as though she was ready to kill him.

'Nothing!' Tammy pushed out vehemently, desperate to end this awful scene. 'We just have very different values.'

'Well, maybe your value has risen in the past four months,' Lucy said.

'I doubt it!' A hysterical little laugh erupted from her throat. 'Sorry for creating. It was a shock. I didn't expect to ever see him again.'

'There's nothing to be sorry about,' Kirsty assured her with another shoulder hug. 'Just remember you have us here if nothing changes for you. Okay?'

Tammy nodded.

'Well, if that was Fletcher landing, he'd better get a move on to join the rest of the guests because it's almost time for us to get going,' Jennifer said briskly. As chief bridesmaid for Lucy, she'd been keeping their preparations on schedule all day. 'Better pick up our bouquets now and remember to hold them at waist level,' she instructed, waving to the bed where the bouquets were laid out ready for them.

It was the last mention of Fletcher, much to Tammy's relief. Still, she felt so rattled by the news he was a guest here at Lucy's wedding, she could barely keep her mind on the proceedings. Luckily, she was the third bridesmaid in the wedding procession, so it was a relatively simple matter to follow the two in front of her and the practice of the previous two weddings held her in good stead. Her feet didn't falter on the long red carpet laid out between the rows of chairs in the courtyard. Kirsty directly preceded her and she kept her eyes trained on her friend's back. She reached the pergola and took her place without mishap. Only then did she let herself think about Fletcher Stanton.

How should she handle it if he approached her again, showed interest again? Had he seized on the neutral ground of this wedding to assess her response to him, whether she might now accept his proposition? Did he still want her so much he was prepared to risk another rejection? Or might he even change his proposition?

How would he react to hearing she was pregnant with his child?

That was the major question.

She shouldn't be thinking of the other issues between them.

His response to her pregnancy would colour everything else.

After the ceremony the wedding party formed a semi-circle behind Lucy and Tony while families and guests lined up to congratulate the newly wedded couple, kissing and shaking hands, then milling around afterwards. Tammy didn't look for Fletcher, not wanting him to think she was hanging on his presence. She chatted to Angelo, Tony's youngest brother, who was the groomsman partnering her.

'Oh, Lord! He's brought someone with him!'

Kirsty hissed, swinging an urgent gaze to Tammy. 'Don't look!'

Her heart plummeted. The very slim hope that something good might come out of this meeting died a painful death. 'I told you it was over,' she slung at Kirsty, and to prove it she did look, steeling herself not to be the least bit affected by the sight of Fletcher with another woman.

He was shaking hands with the groom and smiling at the bride. Linked to his other arm was a stunning Junoesque blonde—a tall woman, almost as tall as Fletcher, her long shining hair cut into different curved lengths to frame a perfect face, a fashionable fringe drawing attention to wide-spaced, spectacular light-blue eyes. She had bee-stung lips like Angelina Jolie's and her voluptuously curved body was poured into a strapless scarlet silk sheath. This woman so far outshone her, Tammy felt herself sinking straight into a dark purple night, savagely wishing she could hide there forever.

Pride forced her to turn to Kirsty and say in cynical dismissal, 'Well, he can afford the best.' Then she resumed chatting to Angelo, pretending that nothing momentous had happened.

Angelo had put himself out to be nice to her during yesterday's tour of the vineyard and had also been good company at dinner last night. That might well have been out of a polite sense of duty since she was his partner for the wedding. She hadn't actually sensed he was attracted to her so there seemed no harm in being extra friendly to him now when she desperately needed some cover for the terrible anguish of knowing beyond any doubt that Fletcher had moved on and would certainly not welcome learning that he was the father of her child.

Angelo Andretti was nowhere near as handsome as Fletcher, who would undoubtedly consider him a comedown for Tammy, but she didn't care about that. In fact, he was quite attractive, his hair a mass of tight black curls, his eyes a warm brown, his nose distinctly Roman, declaring his Italian heritage, and he had a happy disposition that made him pleasant company. It was easy to overlook the fact that he was rather short—barely matching Tammy's height in her high heels—and stocky.

As the wedding party moved off to pose in the vineyard, Lucy grabbed her arm and pulled her aside for a quick, confidential tête-à-tête. 'I didn't know Fletcher was bringing a woman with him, Tam. I would have warned you.'

'It doesn't matter, Lucy,' she insisted.

'I just asked Mum about it. He called this morning to check if it was okay for him to bring a partner and she said it would be no problem. I'm so sorry, Tam.'

'Lucy, it's no problem. Please don't worry about me. Let's just enjoy your wedding. Okay?'

Lucy searched her eyes anxiously. 'You sure?'

'I'm sure!' Tammy replied emphatically, forcing a big smile. 'Are we going to frolic amongst the grapes for the photographer?'

Lucy relaxed and grinned back. 'Why not? It's fun time.'

Apparently Kirsty and Lucy passed the word to the gang that she was not upset by the situation because none of the others mentioned Fletcher to her, much to her relief. She did her absolute best to block him out of her mind and float through the evening as though he wasn't there.

She sat beside Angelo at the long bridal table, giving him most of her attention. He was keen for her to sample the wines being served, and she did, though only taking small sips of each one. Eating was difficult but she determinedly forced enough food down to display a reasonably good appetite, not wanting to raise any questions about it. She applauded the speeches, smiled at the comments Angelo whispered in her ear about them, and generally felt that anyone observing her—especially Fletcher—would think she was having a lovely time.

Unfortunately Angelo was not a good dancer. He shuffled through the bridal waltz, twice stepping on her toes during the turns, for which he apologised profusely, making it difficult to ignore his clumsiness. It was obviously a relief to him when the waltz was over and Tammy said she now had the duty of serving the wedding cake, which excused him from having to continue dancing with her.

The DJ was inviting guests to join the bridal couple on the dance floor as she and Angelo left it, and suddenly there was Fletcher, walking directly towards her with the blonde's arm hooked around his. Trying to avoid him would indicate that his presence with another woman had hurt her. Defence mechanisms instantly kicked in as the distance between them closed and *he* made no move to avoid her. She held her head high, looked at him with a curious air as though wondering why she had ever found him attractive, and when they were virtually face-to-face, pasted a dry little smile on her lips.

'Surprise, surprise!' she said sardonically. 'You seem doomed to be hooked into my friends' weddings, Fletcher.'

His eyes burned into hers. 'Any chance that you'll be the bride at the fourth, Tamalyn?'

'Who knows?' she said with a shrug, hugging Angelo's arm more tightly as she turned a smile to him. 'This is Celine's brother, Fletcher Stanton, Angelo.'

'And you're the brother of the groom,' Fletcher chimed straight in, thrusting out his hand, which meant Angelo had to detach himself from Tammy to take and shake it. 'Fine vineyard you have here.'

'Thank you. We're proud of it.'

'A wonderful setting for the wedding,' the blonde gushed, her accent distinctly foreign—German? Swiss?

'Heidi Bergman,' Fletcher said in a too-brief introduction, not giving any information about his companion. 'Angelo Andretti and Tamalyn Haynes, Heidi.'

'Hi!' Tammy said as brightly as she could.

'Hope you're enjoying yourself,' Angelo said warmly.

'I am,' the blonde assured him, smiling a row of perfect white teeth.

Tammy barely stopped herself from gnashing hers.

'I haven't been to a wedding for ages,' Heidi directed at her. 'It's so unusual to have five bridesmaids. Fletcher was telling me about your gang-of-six friendship from schooldays. Amazing that the bond has lasted over the years.'

'We work at it,' Tammy said, thinking female friendship probably wasn't high on the list of Heidi Bergman's priorities. Notching up male conquests would be more her style. Or was she being bitchy out of sheer jealousy?

'I imagine you're much in demand for advice with two of the gang pregnant,' Fletcher remarked.

'Oh? Have you already had a baby, Tamalyn?' Heidi leapt in, her fantastic eyes alight with curious interest.

For one vicious moment, Tammy was tempted to drop the bombshell of her pregnancy to Fletcher in both their faces but there was no dignity in that.

'No. I'm a midwife,' she answered, hating the blonde's use of her full name. It had been special to *him*. Not anymore, she told herself savagely.

'A very caring one,' Fletcher said in a soft reminiscent tone that totally gutted her. 'I'm glad Celine has you as her friend.'

'Yes, it must be a relief to you that I'm on hand for her,' Tammy shot at him, her eyes steeled to reject any shred of caring from him.. 'She can hardly lean on an absent brother.'

'I'm sure Andrew provides all the male support Celine needs,' he swiftly asserted.

'Amazing, isn't it? They actually feel confident enough of each other's love to start a family.'

Tammy knew her tongue was running away from any sense of discretion, but she wanted to rip into him, wanted to challenge his cynical sense of values because her instincts were screaming that he *was* her man, her mate, and she hated the power he had to make her feel this.

'No comment?' she ran on, her eyes fiercely challenging his. 'Do you think she's having a baby too soon? That the commitment hasn't been tested long enough yet?'

'What is this?' Angelo broke in, disturbed by the charged air of conflict and not relating to the argument at all. 'Marriage is for family,' he stated with conviction. 'Babies cannot come too soon.'

Obviously not for the Andretti family.

Which was marvellous for Lucy.

Realising she had overstepped what was acceptable to Angelo, Tammy switched on an appeasing smile, turning to him and taking his arm again, squeezing it companionably. 'My sentiments exactly,' she declared. 'I *love* babies.'

'Ah! It will be good for Lucy, too, you being a midwife,' he said with beaming satisfaction.

'She can call me any time,' Tammy avowed, then lifted her smile to Fletcher. 'Silly of me to bring up an old difference of opinion. Do go on and dance.' She even managed to extend the smile to Heidi. 'Have a good time.'

'Thank you.' The golden blonde tugged Fletcher's arm, eager to get him away from the little purple shrew who had stolen his attention. 'Come on. The dance floor is getting crowded.'

He gave Tammy a searing look that said there was unfinished business between them, then moved to oblige his partner.

It was just his arrogance that was pricked, Tammy

told herself, heading off in the opposite direction with Angelo in tow. He wouldn't like being cut off from making any reply to an argument. Not that it was of any real importance to him. And no doubt the sexy blonde would ease whatever niggling frustration had been raised in that brief encounter.

'You've had a previous relationship with Fletcher Stanton?' Angelo inquired as he escorted her over to the table where the cake was being cut.

Tammy instantly shied from getting into that painful subject. 'He was my partner at Celine's wedding where he expressed the opinion that his sister was marrying too young.' She shrugged off the incident, ruefully adding, 'I'm afraid he and I got into an argument about it. Sorry, Angelo. I shouldn't have touched on it again.'

'I felt there was more,' he remarked, slanting her a searching look. 'A connection…'

She tried to laugh it off, airily pointing out, 'He's with another woman.'

'That's true,' he agreed. 'But I think he wants to be with you, Tammy.'

She huffed with mock impatience. 'Now how can you say that? Heidi Bergman is an absolute stunner.'

'Mmm…' He grinned. 'Super show-piece. But he did not feel for her. All his focus was on you.'

'Well, I don't know why.' She shook her head, denying any interest, though her mind was churning with the possibility that Angelo could be right. Hope was a terribly treacherous thing.

'I bet he will seek you out before the night is over.'

She frowned. 'I'm with you, Angelo.' The decision to demonstrate to Fletcher that she wasn't available was still good common sense. She shouldn't let herself be swayed from it by Angelo's observations.

He laughed. 'I'm happy for you to use me as you like, Tammy, but the vibes don't lie. I got the impression you were under his skin and he was under yours, big-time. I won't be offended if you go off with him. I have a lot of family friends here to catch up with.'

They'd reached the cake table, and he gave her a cheery, confidential wink as he left her to her bridesmaid's duty, heading off to the courtyard for the ready company of other guests who had moved out to the cooler night air.

A waitress held out a tray loaded with finger slices of wedding cake wrapped in white paper serviettes. 'This one's ready to go.'

'Thank you.'

Tammy sucked in a deep breath as she took the tray, trying to soothe hopelessly frayed nerves. Her heart was torn with wanting to believe Angelo and knowing no good could come from spending more time with Fletcher. If he had wanted to resume a relationship with her, he wouldn't have brought Heidi Bergman with him. That was clear-cut evidence of where he stood.

She didn't need this turbulent ambivalence.

If Fletcher did seek her out for some private togetherness, she would tell him she was pregnant with his child.

That would certainly be make-or-break time.

CHAPTER NINE

WITH all the official wedding business done, it was well and truly party time. The DJ played a great selection of dance music, and Tammy heartily wished Angelo didn't have two left feet. She loved dancing, always had. Ballet, tap, contemporary jazz, ballroom—she'd had lessons in them all throughout her childhood and adolescence—lessons in every activity—swimming, tennis, even golf—whatever kept her occupied away from home and her mother's social orbit.

Latin American was her favourite, but she was happy doing any form of dance. Tonight of all nights, it would have helped if she'd been able to lose herself in the music. In fact, it was difficult not to keep tapping her feet to the beat as she sat out in the courtyard, chatting with a group of Tony's friends. It was even more difficult not to think about Fletcher being hot to trot with Heidi Bergman on the dance floor.

She didn't want to see them so she didn't look; though, out of sight, out of mind, was not working too well for her. Nevertheless, her determination to concentrate on being responsive to the company she was in, had her laughing at one of Angelo's jokes so hard, she wasn't aware of Fletcher's approach to their corner of the courtyard.

'I won the bet, Tammy,' Angelo said, winking triumphantly at her.

For a moment she was confused over what he was talking about, thinking the comment was somehow linked to the joke he'd just told. Then Fletcher's voice sent a frisson of shock down her spine.

'Pardon me for interrupting the jollity,' he said in a tone that smacked of good humour but had a slight edge to it. 'May I steal your partner for a dance, Angelo?'

'Be glad if you would. I'm sure Tammy would enjoy dancing with someone who can,' Angelo said straight out with an invitational gesture.

'Oh, truly! It doesn't matter!' she cried in pleading protest, her body instantly abuzz with rioting hormones at the prospect of close physical contact with Fletcher.

'Go on, have fun,' Angelo urged, a mischievous grin on his face.

'You owe me this dance, Tamalyn,' Fletcher claimed, arrogantly demanding her compliance.

She wheeled on him, chin up in proud defiance, eyes flaring a fierce challenge. 'No, I don't! I don't owe you anything!'

'The salsa at Celine's wedding?' he reminded her, one black eyebrow raised in counter-challenge. 'You ducked out on it to look after a sick child.'

'That was then,' she argued. *This is now and you've got Heidi Bergman as your partner.*

'Don't be churlish, Tamalyn. A promise is a promise.'

Churlish!

Her cheeks burned as the realisation hit her she must have sounded like that to everyone in earshot.

He reached out and took her hand in an iron grip. 'Come on,' he commanded, his eyes boring into hers with ruthless intent, *promising* he wasn't about to go away, no matter what she said or did.

Short of making a horribly embarrassing scene, it was impossible not to go with him. 'I'll be back soon,' she threw at Angelo who looked vastly amused by the situation.

'Take your time. No hurry,' he blithely replied.

The strong hand pulling hers forced her to fall into step with Fletcher as he led her off towards the dance floor in the middle of the restaurant. Seething with resentment at his alpha male domination act, she muttered, 'I didn't promise you anything and you know it.'

'*I* did. To dance you off your feet.' He slanted her a look that blazed with unshakeable purpose. 'And I'm in the mood to do it.'

'Why?' she snapped. 'Can't Heidi satisfy you?'

'Not with you stuck in my mind.'

The savage retort took her breath away. A treacherous pleasure raced through her. She tried to put a stop to it with the obvious truth that he didn't *want* her stuck in his mind, but there was a very primitive satisfaction in knowing that not even the beautiful and sexy Heidi Bergman could displace whatever he felt for her. Though it wouldn't do her any good since he didn't like acknowledging it.

The rock music being played came to an end and many couples were leaving the dance floor for a breather as Fletcher virtually pulled her towards it. Heidi was amongst them, being led to the open bar by a man Tammy didn't recognise—a guest she didn't know. Had Fletcher seized the break from his chosen partner to seek her out or had he manipulated it? How much pulling power did she have?

Tantalising thought…

'Too late,' she said, waving at the departing couples, wondering what he would do next to keep her with him without music to dance to.

'No. It's perfect timing,' he claimed, shooting her a glittering glance that denied her any escape.

He raised his arm, apparently a pre-arranged

signal to the DJ who obligingly announced, 'I've had a request for a few Latin American numbers, starting off with the salsa.'

'You organised this?' she cried, stunned at the extent he had gone to in order to have her to himself for a few minutes.

Again the arched eyebrow, challenging her to perform for him. 'Did you lie about its being your favourite?'

'No. I'll dance *you* off *your* feet.'

'Do try,' he retorted with a wolfish grin, sweeping her onto the dance floor and into his arms as the music started to pump out its seductive beat.

She did try, anger sizzling through the heat he stirred with his blatantly sexy moves. She twirled, she shimmied, she played the provocative tease to the hilt, wanting him to burn with desire for her, wanting to scorch his mind with a memory he couldn't evict, brand it on his soul so that no other woman could ever interest him. Be damned if she'd let him find solace for his needs with other Heidi Bergmans! She'd found no solace for hers.

He more than matched everything she did, taking command with masterful expertise, bending her over his arm, his muscular thighs pressed hard against hers in support, swirling her into lifts which then forced her to slide down him in full body contact, her breasts squashing against the strong wall of his chest. And he had rhythm in spades, his feet as agile as hers, the sway of his body so animal-sexy it was mesmerising, in constant counter-challenge to hers.

The other couples cleared the floor, watching them, clapping to the beat. They were putting on a show. Tammy didn't care who saw them. Apparently Fletcher didn't, either. They were consumed by the dance, consumed by each other, eye contact transmitting every ounce of the passion they were putting into expressing feelings that were not going to be acknowledged any other way.

Pride forbade her to beg anything of him. He'd already made it clear that he was not here to make any commitment to a relationship with her. This— what was pounding through them, pouring between them—he probably viewed as an aberration. He still had Heidi Bergman waiting in the wings, preventing him from taking a step too far beyond the dance floor. There was only this.

It ended in a clinch, her body pinned to his by a clamping arm, both of them breathing hard, chests heaving, eyes blazing with aggressive primal instincts. Spectators' applause crashed around them. For several highly charged moments, Fletcher held her tight, his gaze simmering down to her panting mouth. Then his fingers dug into her waist and he swung her out of his embrace to face the crowd of people encircling the dance floor, still clapping and calling out, 'Bravo!'

Somehow Tammy seized the presence of mind to drop into a curtsey as though she'd just given a professional performance. Fletcher instantly took his cue from her, bowing and waving her upright again.

'More, more!'

It was Angelo calling out, clapping his hands over his head and grinning from ear to ear.

'No! Enough!' Tammy said decisively. What she felt with Fletcher Stanton was not a spectator sport. She turned to him, working her mouth into a coolly appreciative smile. 'Thank you. I have to concede you did dance me off my feet. Please excuse me now.'

'Cha-cha coming up,' the DJ announced.

'Tamalyn…' It was a gruff, gut-wrenching demand for her to stay.

'You brought a partner with you,' she tersely reminded him as the music started up again.

'And if I hadn't?' he parried—a strike below the belt, delivered with a tense air of recklessness that had Tammy hesitating, unsure if he was actually prepared to dump Heidi to be with her.

'You made a choice. Deal with it,' she shot at him.

Other dancers were moving onto the floor. She wriggled her hand free of his and dived between two couples, so churned up inside that escape was her only thought. Angelo was standing somewhere on the sideline. He had got her into this. He had to get her out.

Before she could reach him, an arm hooked around her waist and she was scooped hard against Fletcher's side, forced to match steps with him as he virtually marched her away from everyone else, taking her towards the verandah at the opposite end of the restaurant to the court-yard—the verandah that overlooked the vineyard. The shock of his abrupt abduction turned her legs to jelly, her stomach to mush. Only her heart seemed to have any strength, hammering with an intensity that didn't allow any sensible thought to enter her mind.

Out on the verandah, heading for the far end where the light from the restaurant didn't reach, where no wedding guests could readily see them. Tammy sucked in the cool night air, an insistent thread of sanity telling her she had to say some-thing, needing breath to do it. She couldn't just let him carry her away like this.

'What…what do you think you're doing?'

As a protest it was hopelessly weak, her voice shaking from the tempest inside her…excitement, fear, anger, all speared through with a terrible yearning for Fletcher to say something that would make it possible for her to tell him about the baby, and give her hope that somehow everything could turn out right between them.

'Taking what I want.'

He swung her into his embrace, slamming her against him, leaving no space for her to try to push away. His mouth crashed down on hers, intent on passionate plunder, and any idea of resistance collapsed in Tammy's mind. The intimate invasion of his tongue triggered a wild outburst of need in her.

Heidi Bergman was totally forgotten. This man was hers. A primitive sense of possession seized her and her arms wound around his waist, hugging hard. He sucked on her lips. His tongue scoured her palate for every taste of her. And she did the same, months of hunger pouring into kiss after kiss. Her body strained even closer to his, wanting the power of his strong maleness to flow into her, exulting in the erection that was furrowing her stomach. His hands slid down the pit of her back, clutched the soft cheeks of her bottom, lifted her into a more sexual fit with him. She was aching for him.

His mouth broke from hers, words jerking out in rasping urgency. 'We have to move from here. You must have a room.'

Her head whirled. A room...yes...but it was shared with Jennifer and Hannah. Were they likely to go there while the party was still raging? The door could be locked. They'd left the key hidden in a pot plant so any one of them could get in at any time. The fever in her blood demanded *this* time with him.

There was a flight of steps down to ground level at the end of the verandah. They could go without being seen, have the privacy needed. She unwound one arm from him to wave at the steps. 'This way.' And afterwards, when everything felt good between them—if it did—she would tell him about the baby. Their baby.

He swept her towards the steps in a rush of eagerness, then halted on the edge of the verandah, holding her back, his hand lifting to grip her chin, turn her face to his. His eyes warred between lust on fire and enforced restraint.

'Tamalyn, are you still on the pill?'

Pill...the pill that hadn't worked. 'No. No, I'm not.' She wasn't yet prepared to say it was impossible to prevent a pregnancy that already existed.

'Damn, damn, damn!' he cursed in furious frustration, shaking his head in anguished denial. 'I didn't bring any protection, didn't plan for this. Can't take the risk.'

Of course not, flashed into her mind, a cold steely shaft of painful truth. A pregnancy would force him into a relationship that was not on his terms, burden

him with a commitment he didn't want. She'd been
a fool to think, even for one moment, that having sex
with him would change anything.

'Better go back to Heidi,' spilled out of her
mouth on a wave of bitterness. 'I bet she's all
geared up to take you on.'

She wrenched her chin out of his grip and
stepped back, pushing his other arm away from her.

'No, wait!'

He caught her hands, kneading her palms with
his thumbs, clearly in some agitation of spirit. She
faced him belligerently, her eyes demanding why
she should wait. His jaw was clenched, his eyes
stormy, his mouth no longer soft and sensual, lips
drawn into a compressed line.

'Heidi…' he bit out. 'She's nothing to me, nor I
to her. She's the sister of my German colleague. In
Sydney on some modelling job. It's her first time
in Australia. Hans asked me to call her, give her
some back-up if she had any problems. I invited her
to the wedding because I wanted to goad some
reaction out of you, Tamalyn.'

'What? By showing that *I* meant nothing to you?'

'That's what you've been doing to me,' he
flashed back at her. 'And it's a lie. We both know
it's a lie now, don't we? You want me as much as
I want you.'

She shook her head. They were back to where

she'd walked away from him on Lord Howe Island. 'I never said I didn't want you, Fletcher. It was your next-step plan I didn't like.'

'Okay. Let's negotiate on that,' he said quickly. 'What inducements can I offer that would make coming to live with me acceptable to you?'

Tammy inwardly recoiled from the situation he still wanted with her, but she didn't instantly reject it this time. She was pregnant with his child. Her life was heading down a different course now. Yet if he didn't want the baby, didn't want the responsibility of being a father, there was no way she could spend any part of her life with him.

'I don't think it's a good idea to make any decisions tonight,' she temporised. 'There are…other considerations.'

He frowned. 'If you mean Heidi…'

'Yes.' She snatched at the diversion. 'You must have made some arrangement to accompany her back to Sydney.'

He grimaced. 'A limousine at midnight.'

'The whole gang is staying here until tomorrow,' she rattled on. 'We won't be leaving until after brunch. Then the drive home will take…'

'You'll have time for me tomorrow night,' he cut in, his eyes glittering anticipation for the pleasures of their next meeting.

'You can come to my apartment at North Sydney

f you like,' she invited, needing to be on her home ground if they were to meet.

'I like.' He grinned and moved to draw her into his embrace again.

Tammy resisted, pushing her hands against his chest, her gaze meeting his in direct challenge. It had to be said and she was acutely aware that any future with him was now hanging on a knife's edge. 'You might not "like," Fletcher, and I'll quite understand if you don't turn up.'

'Nothing will keep me away,' he scoffed with arrogant confidence. No doubt he was already planning to buy a stack of condoms.

'There's something I want you to think about in the meantime,' she warned.

'Lay it out,' he invited, not the slightest crack in his confidence.

Her heart ached with the question of whether he had any love for her or simply wanted desire and ego satisfied. Tammy took a deep breath and pleaded, 'I don't want a scene here and now, Fletcher. It's Lucy's wedding, and nothing you say will make any difference to the fact. I'm going to tell you something, then return to the wedding party and leave you to think about it. You may or may not want to reconnect with me tomorrow night. That's up to you. Okay?'

He frowned, sensing how deeply serious she

was. 'Tamalyn…there's nothing you can say that I won't find a way around.'

She pushed one hand up from his chest and laid her fingers across his lips, then forced out the make or break words, her eyes begging him to believe her. 'I didn't plan this, Fletcher. I took the pill, just as I was instructed to. No mistakes. I was the unlucky one or two percent in the failure statistics.'

'What?' Shock in his voice; shock stamped on his face; eyes stunned, losing their sharp focus on her.

'I'm four months' pregnant,' she stated quietly. 'I *will* have the baby, so don't come to me suggesting an abortion. Don't come to me at all if you don't want any part of fatherhood because the baby and I…we're a package deal.'

He shook his head as though it was reeling. He really had been hit byaJohn…no one could make anything nasty out of that name at school. Whether or not he'd been born a genius—it was too early to tell—Fletcher was determined on protecting their child from any avoidable hurt. Thunderbolt this time, and not one he could ever have anticipated.

She touched his cheek in a wry farewell. 'I won't come after you for anything, Fletcher. You're free to make whatever choice you want to make. I hope I see you tomorrow night, but if I don't…this really is goodbye.'

There was no reaction from him as she moved

away, forcing herself to walk back down the verandah. She wasn't sure how much of what she'd said had sunk in beyond the fact of her pregnancy, didn't know if his mind was processing it all or shut down with shock.

'Tamalyn…' It was a harsh command for her to halt.

She was almost at the entry into the restaurant. The force of his willpower slammed into her heart, but her mind still insisted on a time delay before any more was said between them.

She paused, looked back. He stood where she'd left him, though he'd swung around to watch her.

'Tomorrow, Fletcher,' she said with unwavering conviction, though her own deep uncertainty about his response made her add, 'If there is one for us.'

Then she quickly faced forward and made her feet walk her back to the wedding party.

CHAPTER TEN

AT MIDNIGHT, with Heidi Bergman in tow, Fletcher took his leave of the bride and groom and their respective families. He had not attempted another private tête-à-tête with Tammy and she had kept well away from him, but she did surreptitiously watch his departure, her heart heavy as she wondered if this was her last sight of him.

As soon as he was gone, the whole gang, led by the bride herself, swooped on her en masse. 'Was I right or was I right?' Lucy crowed in triumphant delight. 'That red-hot salsa gave it away, Tammy.'

'Not to mention the long private time out on the verandah,' Hannah swiftly inserted.

'None of us were fooled for a minute when he returned to the blonde. He looked so tense and distracted he could barely give her polite attention,' Jennifer said with satisfaction.

'I bet you told him he had to finish with her before you'd see him again,' Kirsty put in gleefully.

'Something like that,' Tammy conceded.

'I love it!' Celine declared. 'My on-top-of-the-world brother couldn't hold on to his huge pride, despite using a show-piece girlfriend to pretend he didn't care. He just had to go after you. And did you stick it to him with that salsa! It was marvellous, Tam. Truly marvellous!'

'So…have you made any definite arrangement for a future meeting?' Lucy demanded to know. 'I'm going to miss out on all this new development, being away on my honeymoon. You can at least tell me that much.'

Tammy shrugged, not wanting to make too big a point of what might never happen. 'I said he could call on me at home tomorrow night.'

They all whooped and clapped and obviously felt enormously pleased with themselves for *knowing* this should be the right outcome. Lucy called out to a waiter, 'Champagne, champagne, more celebration over here!'

Tammy said nothing to spoil the happy, ebullient mood. It was right for Lucy's wedding. The fact that any development between her and Fletcher hung on her pregnancy could be kept to a later date. The only thing she was sure of—and it was a very real comfort—was the gang's support, regardless of what happened with Fletcher. She wouldn't be alone with her pregnancy. They'd keep her in a tight loop with them, caring and sharing as they always had.

It was after one o'clock in the afternoon by the time they left the Andretti vineyard the next day, Hannah and Tammy travelling with Jennifer in her car, Celine and Kirsty, of course, leaving separately with their respective husbands.

'Three weddings down and three to go,' Hannah remarked as they headed back to Sydney. 'We've got Tam and Fletcher together again, which is very promising.'

'I think you're jumping the gun there,' Tammy quickly warned.

Jennifer threw her a grin. 'Not from where we see it. The hook is definitely in.'

Tammy winced at that description, knowing it was probably how Fletcher thought of her pregnancy. Needing to divert her friends from pursuing an analysis of her situation, she pushed for a different subject. 'What about you, Jen? I thought you were really tight with Adam but you didn't ask him to Lucy's wedding.'

Jennifer heaved a deep sigh. 'I did, but he didn't want to take the time off writing. Everything's been on hold this past month and will continue to be until the book is done. He's on a tight deadline for delivering this second one and he's cloistered himself up in his cottage at Leura to get it written.

I only see him when he needs a breather from it. Mind you, I understand…'

She rattled on about the publishing industry, how it was best to capitalise on the reader interest created by a first-book bestseller, the need to produce something just as sensational—pressure, pressure, pressure.

When Jennifer ran out of steam, Hannah confided that she had recently met a man whom she found very attractive. He owned and ran a sports store at Terrigal—a beach resort on the Central Coast where Hannah's mother had gone to live after the divorce from her husband three years ago. They'd only had minimal contact, since she lived and worked in Sydney, but on her last weekend visit to her mother…

Tammy's mind drifted away from the conversation. Hannah and Jennifer occupied the front seats of the car, she the back, and they didn't require any active participation from her, happy to burble on to each other. They probably knew she wanted to think about Fletcher and were leaving her to it. Not that thinking about him would help anything.

She kept remembering his words: 'There's nothing you can say that I won't find a way around.'

Fletcher didn't like being defeated. He was used to winning.

He saw her as a challenge.

Maybe he would view fatherhood as a challenge, too.

Or he could see the whole thing as calculated entrapment which he would absolutely refuse to be a victim of in any shape or form.

Sunday-afternoon traffic was slow. It was four-thirty by the time they reached North Sydney. 'Good luck!' both Jennifer and Hannah chorussed as she alighted from the car in front of her apartment block.

'He might not come,' she tossed at them.

'He'll come!' they asserted in unison.

She managed a laugh and waved them off, wishing she had their confidence. Though hope did soar as she entered her studio apartment and heard the telephone ringing. Dropping her bag, she raced to the kitchenette counter and snatched up the receiver, then tried not to sound too breathless as she identified herself to the caller.

'Tammy Haynes.'

'You're finally home. I'll be there in ten minutes.'

Fletcher's voice. No doubt about that. Very terse in tone. And he ended the call without asking if ten minutes would be convenient to her. Clearly he was not big on patience, and the word *finally* suggested he'd already called several times and been frustrated by not getting a reply.

Not that any of those things were particularly relevant.

He was coming.

After all her mental turmoil and heartache about the situation between them, Tammy suddenly felt weirdly numb. In a mechanical daze, she returned to her bag, picked it up, took it into her small bedroom, left it by her clothes cupboard, visited the bathroom, spent a minute or two staring blankly at herself in the vanity mirror before remembering to tidy her hair and refresh her lipstick, then went back to the kitchenette and sat on the bar-stool to wait until Fletcher arrived.

He was coming.

The father of her child.

And he'd tell her what he wanted to do about it.

She didn't have to think about anything until he gave her that information.

The doorbell rang.

A few seconds later she was face-to-face with the man who had already changed her life with the conception of their child. Somehow whatever other changes he had in mind seemed like relatively minor things to consider.

His eyes seared hers with burning determination. 'You can't turn away from me now, Tamalyn.'

'No,' she agreed, stepping back to wave him in.

His gaze dropped to her stomach. 'You don't look pregnant. Shouldn't you have a bit of a pot belly by four months?' he said, frowning at her as though she wasn't doing things right.

'It depends on body type,' Tammy said with calm authority. 'And some women pile on more weight than they should, giving themselves the licence of eating for two. It's better to watch your diet, keep fit and healthy.'

'Well, you should know,' he muttered, and stepped past her into the apartment.

She closed the door and leaned back against it, staying out of the firing line of the volatile aggression pouring from him as he stalked around, checking out her living space, even poking his head into her bedroom and bathroom. 'This is a shoebox, Tamalyn,' he shot at her.

Her chin rose defensively. 'I've managed here quite happily for the past seven years.'

'It meets a single person's needs. It will not do for you and the baby,' he stated emphatically, his gaze dropping to her stomach again. 'Are we having a son or a daughter?'

'I don't know yet. I'm booked in for an ultrasound this week. That's when…if you want to know…'

'Right! I'll go with you. We'll find out together.'

He scooped up her door key and the handbag she had laid on the kitchenette counter when she'd grabbed for the telephone. 'Let's move,' he said with an air of unassailable decision, striding back to her and gathering her in to his side as he reopened the door.

'Where are you taking me?' she asked, alarm at being swept out of the security of her own home kicking her heart out of its numb state.

'I'm taking you to what will be *our* place.'

He scooped her out of *her* place, locked the door on it and held on to the key and her handbag as he forcefully escorted her out of the apartment building. Tammy didn't resist, didn't protest, either. Her pulse was pounding at her temples as her mind tried to come to grips with what he was telling her.

He wasn't just staying in Sydney for the ultrasound but acquiring a place for them to live in? Did he mean to give up his work overseas and settle here now? Was fatherhood so important to him? He seemed to have completely dismissed any suspicion that she might have tricked him into it. Which was a huge relief. She would have hated that reaction, would have rejected having anything to do with him under that cloud.

Perhaps his super-brain had told him to bypass it as destructive material which would not get him what he wanted. He'd obviously planned several initiatives since last night and was swamping any possible negativity from her with sheer ruthless speed of action. She barely had time to note that the silver car he was leading her to was not a Porsche. It had the stylish lines of a luxury sedan.

'Have you gone off sports cars?' she asked as he opened the front passenger door for her.

'This is a more suitable family car,' he answered. 'The Lexus GS450H, a petrol/electric hybrid with green credentials second to none—great fuel economy, low emissions, whisper-quiet efficiency. It's the benchmark in social responsibility for other car manufacturers. You're stepping into the future, Tamalyn.'

She had a far more personal future tearing at her mind. 'My bag and key, please,' she demanded before stepping into the car, needing to have some means of independence in this power-play from Fletcher. She couldn't quite bring herself to believe he intended them to be a proper family, despite the sudden acquisition of a family car.

He passed over her handbag and door key and she settled on the passenger seat. As he closed the door she was wondering just how far ahead his planning went.

'Like it?' he asked as he took the driver's seat.

'Very classy,' she answered.

'It took the prize for best luxury car this year,' he informed her, starting the engine which *was* whisper quiet compared to the Porsche.

'I can see why.' Everything inside the car shouted highest-scale luxury. Any other time she might have enjoyed riding in it, but today… 'Precisely where are you taking me, Fletcher?'

The thought of being too far from her apartment to easily bolt home stirred a panic attack. She should not have let herself be drawn into a trip that might make everything more difficult.

'Just down to Blues Point. Only take ten minutes.'

His reply eased some of her inner tension. Such a short distance was walkable. Fletcher kept pointing out the special features of the car as he drove, apparently wanting her impressed with its clever technology and its fantastic inbuilt safety measures. The words floated over Tammy's head, not sinking in. She didn't take any notice of where they were travelling, either, until Fletcher turned the car into a garage driveway, activating the security door with a remote control.

Startled, she looked up at a huge block of apartments just before he drove into a basement carpark. 'You've rented a place here?'

'No.' He flashed a winning grin at her as he brought the car to a halt beside an elevator. 'I've started the process of buying one here.'

'When?' The stunned question spilled from her lips.

'It was shown to me this morning.'

He was out of the car before she could find wits

enough to question him further, bounding around it to open her door and help her out. The moment she was on her feet, he linked her arm with his, slammed the car door shut and placed a finger to her lips to prevent her asking for more information. 'Wait!' he commanded. 'I want you to see.'

He looked both arrogantly sure of himself and brimming with barely contained excitement. Tammy kept her mouth shut, his confidence and high spirits fuelling a growing excitement in her. Maybe she was worrying for nothing. A home in Sydney, a family car, an interest in fatherhood…

Fletcher hugged her arm tightly, possessively, as he led her to the elevator. She didn't see what button he pressed. The doors closed and he swept her into his embrace as the compartment began to rise.

'I told you I'd give you anything you wanted, Tamalyn,' he said, then kissed her, and kept kissing her until the elevator came to a halt.

Tammy was giddy with wildly impassioned pleasure as he swept her out to a lobby and straight to a door which he quickly unlocked and thrust wide open, stepping inside and scooping her with him. She was instantly stunned by a 180-degree view of Sydney Harbour—the great coathanger bridge towering over the gleaming white sails of the opera house, Darling Harbour, Anzac bridge, the skyline of the city, the whole expanse of sparkling blue water and the boats and ferries making their white tracks over it.

'Remember at Kirsty's wedding you said there was more spectacular beauty here than anywhere else in the world? Well, now we have it to ourselves,' Fletcher said with triumphant satisfaction.

She shook her head in amazement, walking dazedly towards the fantastic wall of glass that encompassed a luxury-packed living area; white leather lounges, glass tables on white marble blocks, beautiful large mats patterned in shades of turquoise, blue and aqua on the gleaming white tiled floor. Her hands gestured helplessly at the fabulous furnishings.

'How did you get all this done?'

'The vendors have bought elsewhere. They wanted this apartment sold as it is—lock, stock and barrel.' He waved dismissively. 'But if this decor is not to your taste, we can replace it with whatever you do like.'

He said it so carelessly, money no object. Of course, it couldn't be. He was a billionaire. Strange how that had never been quite real to her. Only the man had ever mattered. But this apartment certainly hit her in the face with his enormous wealth. It must have cost him many millions. And suggesting the option of refurnishing to her taste... *I'll give you anything you want, Tamalyn.*

Except not once had he mentioned love.

Was she ready to accept being a rich man's mistress if it meant having Fletcher in her life for at least part of their child's upbringing? Would parenthood bond them together beyond the sexual desire that could be all too short-lived?

'I thought you'd like the blues,' he pressed. 'It's your colour.'

'Everything is beautiful. I love the blues,' she said, waving to the mats and the matching cushions on the lounges. Though she wasn't sure how a baby would fit in here. This was clearly not designed as a family residence, more a marvellous show-piece for high-flying career people or celebrity socialites. She wasn't sure she fitted in here, being neither, but Fletcher did, and she could probably weave her own life around his.

'I've negotiated a short-term lease until the sale contract goes through. We can move in right now,' he said with an air of determined purpose. 'In fact, my gear is already in the master bedroom. We can fetch yours tomorrow.'

It was one push too far for Tammy. What he'd already set in place was incredibly impressive and persuasive, but if he thought she would discard the life she'd worked for to suit his time-table, he could think again. 'I'm due to work a shift at the hospital tomorrow, Fletcher. On Tuesday and Wednesday, as well. Thursday is my next day off,' she said, her eyes fiercely denying him any authority over her.

His eyes narrowed into hard probing slits, assessing the strength of the line she had just drawn. The air between them began to seethe with tension, but Tammy refused to back down on this point. He could shower her with all the material possessions in the world. She would not surrender her whole life to him for his convenience.

'There's not much *give* in you, is there, Tamalyn?' he said with biting irony.

She felt her cheeks bloom with heat. 'Not much *take* in me, either,' she fired back at him. 'You won't find me an expensive mistress to keep.'

His mouth curled sardonically as he walked towards her. 'We've moved past the live-in lover proposition. We have a completely different situation to deal with. You're expecting my child.'

She gestured around her in confused appeal. 'Then what is this all about?'

He caught her hands, threading his fingers through hers and gripping hard as he lifted the locked contact up between her breasts and his chest. There was a dark fire in his eyes, burning a challenge directly into hers.

'We get married, Tamalyn,' he said in a soft, infinitely dangerous tone. 'Isn't that what you want most of all?'

CHAPTER ELEVEN

TAMMY stared at him in horror as her mind reeled from what he meant. Marriage…an ambition. Achieving it by deliberately getting pregnant. Nothing to do with love. Nothing…

Her face went cold, clammy. She wasn't conscious of her blood draining from it, wasn't conscious of blacking out, falling. The next thing she was whoozily aware of was being carried. She struggled to understand. 'What…?'

'You fainted,' Fletcher said tersely, setting her down on the edge of a bed. 'Put your head down between your knees, Tamalyn.'

She did as instructed, shocked that her body had shut down on her. The only time she'd fainted before was when she'd got her first period. Was she bleeding, having a miscarriage? There was no feeling of wetness, no draggy feeling in her abdomen, just dizziness in her head.

'Deep breaths,' Fletcher commanded.

The moment of panic receded. She took deep breaths and the dizziness receded, too. Fletcher had seated himself beside her, his arm around her shoulders, holding her, keeping her pressed down.

'I'm okay now,' she choked out.

'Sure?'

'Yes.'

He stood her on her feet, one arm still around her shoulders in strong support as he flung the doona on the bed aside and pulled pillows into a heap for comfortable back support. 'You sit here and rest.' He lifted her into the position he'd arranged and tucked the doona around her. 'I'll go and fix you something to drink and eat.'

Tammy was grateful for the time alone to take stock of the situation and decide what she should do. It was very seductive having a strong man looking after her, caring for her needs, and right now she felt too weak to get up and go anywhere.

Fletcher had carried her into what was obviously the master bedroom. It was incredibly spacious. A wall of glass showcased the view again and the blue-and-white decor was repeated—thick white carpet on the floor, and the doona was blue silk, printed with beautiful water-lilies. On the white bedside tables were fascinating lamps shaped like silver trees with crystal leaves in shades of blue and pink and green and tiny light globes set in the branches. She wondered what they would look like turned on at night.

The desire to spend the night with Fletcher—take what she could—rolled through her like a tidal wave of need. But she couldn't marry him, knowing how he saw it, and wishing wouldn't make it any different. It was impossible to overlook the slur on her integrity, impossible to live with him unless there was respect on both sides.

He strode back into the bedroom, carrying a plate of raisin toast and a glass of orange juice. Tammy's pulse instantly quickened at his air of determined purpose, his dark gaze scanning her face with sharp intensity. 'You still look too pale,' he observed as he set the refreshments down on the bedside table.

'I won't marry you, Fletcher,' she stated decisively.

'Oh, yes, you will,' he fiercely retorted, his eyes stabbing into hers as though he'd pin her to a wall until she agreed to it. 'You're light-headed right now, not thinking straight. Eat, Tamalyn. Then we'll talk.'

'You believe I planned to get pregnant,' she fired at him, refusing to be dominated or intimidated, though the force of his will was making her feel weak and shaky.

'No, I don't,' he shot straight back.

'Then why did you say…?'

'Never mind what I said.' He cut the air with his hand, wanting the issue dismissed.

'I do mind. I mind very much. It's not my ambition to marry you.'

His eyes seethed with black resentment at her stubborn attitude. 'I don't know what the hell drives you,' he bit out angrily. 'I've never met a woman even remotely like you. But we are going to have a child and we have to consider—both of us—what's best for the child. And right at this minute—' he shook a finger at her '—it's best that you eat. So do it!'

He didn't wait for her to obey, swinging away from the bed and striding over to the wall of glass, standing there with his hands slung on his hips, looking out, though Tammy suspected he wasn't seeing anything. His back was rigid with determination, and no doubt his mind was ticking through ways to get past her resistance.

She reached for a piece of toast. Her hand was trembling. The need to regain some strength forced her to eat and drink. Best to calm down, as well, she told herself. Stress wasn't good for the baby. She munched through the raisin toast, washed it down with the sweet orange juice and did feel better for it, more settled for listening to what Fletcher had on his mind.

'Plate and glass empty,' she said, wanting him to

enlighten her on his motives for marriage, since he'd just back-tracked on what were supposed to be hers.

He turned slowly, tension carving his handsome face into hard lines and emanating so powerfully from him, Tammy hugged herself in self-protective comfort, instinctively warding off the sense of attack coming at her.

'I won't let you shut me out of your life,' he threw at her grimly. 'As the father of our child, I have legal rights and I'll claim them.'

She took a deep breath to ease the tightness in her chest and said, 'I don't want to shut you out, Fletcher, and I readily concede you have rights. I'll always respect them.'

'Words!' he scoffed. 'I won't settle for anything less than a guaranteed situation. A contract, signed and sealed.'

His absolute insistence on a contract seemed totally unreasonable. 'How involved do you want to be in our child's life?' she asked, wanting some idea of the depth and breadth of his commitment to fatherhood.

'I will not have arbitrary limitations put upon my involvement,' he threw at her in savage dismissal of any terms she might suggest. 'I have to be there for my child, to stop what will happen if I'm not.'

Tammy shook her head, not understanding his

vehement claim. 'What do you think will happen? I promise you, I'll love our child whether you're there or not.'

'But you're not *me,* Tamalyn,' he mocked. 'And no-one who hasn't been born a child prodigy can imagine what it's like to be one.'

It was a jolt, hearing him describe himself in those terms. But, of course, he had been a prodigy, a super-brain at mathematics from a very early age. Not once had she connected that fact to the baby in her womb, and it stunned her to realise that he had, seeing it as an issue of prime importance.

'I think you'll be a very loving mother,' he conceded, a wry twist on his lips. 'It's in your nature to be, and if love were enough...' He shook his head. 'It's not. When no one in your family has any empathy with how your mind works, the loneliness of it kills off the sense of being loved.'

Loneliness...she remembered Celine calling him a self-contained beast. Had Fletcher chosen to occupy a world of his own or been driven into that existence by the talent he'd been born with? She stared at him, gathering a completely new perspective of the man—a man alone in a way she had never been alone.

He started pacing around the bedroom like a

caged lion, throwing out pieces of what he had lived with and hated. 'My parents did their best for me. I know they did. It wasn't their fault that I didn't fit in anywhere, that I was taunted at school for being a weird oddity, resented at university for being so young and outshining the older students. I don't blame them for finding Celine so much easier to love. Nothing abnormal about my sister. I was like some cuckoo in their nest, an alien child. No one in my family ever knew how to relate to me.'

She had never felt that—a misfit in the normal stream of humanity—unacceptable by other people. Her parents hadn't wanted her but that was something else. Her nannies had liked her. So had her teachers all through her school years. There never had been any problem with acceptance by her friends or her associates at work.

'Though there are piles of people wanting to relate to me now,' Fletcher added cynically. 'International success and billions of dollars makes what I am inside totally irrelevant to them.'

'Not to me, Fletcher,' Tammy put in quietly.

He halted, swinging around to claw into her. 'The woman who can't be bought. Why not, Tamalyn? What makes you immune to the lure of what you could get out of me?'

Understanding each other was good, Tammy thought. It might lead to trust, which was of prime importance to her. This time she didn't hesitate over laying out the truth of her *family* background. 'It's how my mother works her life. She's obsessed with pursuing wealthy men, acquiring whatever she can get out of them. I've seen how it is…being bought by a man…being discarded when a brighter bauble beckons.' She shook her head. 'I think it's a self-destructive path. I couldn't feel any respect for myself if I took it.'

'Hard to shake a deep imprint,' he bit out in frustration.

'I know I'm capable of looking after myself,' she asserted, flashing him a look of belligerent pride as she added, 'I don't need a man to do it.'

Ruthless purpose slid back into place. 'You pride yourself on your independence, but this is something you can't do alone. You have no idea what you'll be faced with if our child inherits the same genetic pattern that made me a prodigy. You'll fail as a mother if I'm not there to support you, because our child will need me, Tamalyn.'

Failure as a mother… Tammy inwardly recoiled from that thought. If she did have one ambition, it was to be the best mother any child could have. Yet with the details of Fletcher's personal experience ringing through her mind, she didn't feel so confident about dealing with needs she'd never known herself.

'Partners in parenthood,' he pushed at her, his dark eyes blazing conviction that this was how it had to be. 'Marriage is the best set-up for that.'

He started strolling around to her side of the bed and she could feel his indomitable will bearing down on her, demanding her acceptance, dismissing any reluctance on her part to give in to him. Her heart started hammering. She *wanted* to be partners in parenthood with him, but marriage to her was a partnership of love, not one of need.

'You might be disappointed, Fletcher,' she threw at him. 'Our child could turn out to be ordinary like me.'

He kept coming. 'You're not ordinary. You're a long, long way from being ordinary.' He purred the words at her, furring them with desire, deliberately intent on stirring the sexual response he knew he could draw from her.

'That's not the point,' she cried, wanting him, wanting him quite desperately, yet still not prepared to be steam-rollered into sealing a partnership that had been proposed on a possibility, not a certainty.

He slid his hand under the doona and laid it on her stomach, the heat of his palm burning through her clothes. '*My* child, either way,' he asserted.

It was as though he drew a response from the baby in her womb. There was a ripple of movement, like a reaching out to him from under her skin. The ruthlessly intent expression on Fletcher's face broke into a grin of delight.

'My child,' he repeated, more of an awed tone in his voice.

Maybe he would be a good father, 'either way,' Tammy thought on a wild wave of hope.

'Let me see. Let me feel,' he said with eager fervour, and somehow she was powerless to resist as he whipped off the shift dress she'd worn and stripped her of bra and panties. The discarding of his own clothes took only a few seconds. She automatically shifted to give him space on the bed, wanting to share her pregnancy with him, thrilled that he was excited by it.

She wasn't sure afterwards if he'd made love to her or made love to their child. It was completely different to any of the sex they'd had before. There was no feverish passion, no fierce possessiveness, more an overwhelming flow of tenderness that melted her heart, melted every bone in her body and filled her with a warmth that completely banished any sense of loneliness.

He held her in a gentle embrace, stroking her hair, stroking her back, making her feel precious— the vessel holding his child—giving her a sweet sense of sharing and caring. It was good being intimate partners in bed, and partners in parenthood had to be right…at least until it was proved wrong. Fletcher was caught up in this new miracle of life and how it might be. The testing time would come after the baby was born.

'Say you'll marry me,' he murmured, rubbing his cheek over the top of her head.

'Okay. I'll marry you,' she said on a sigh of surrender.

He instantly rolled her onto her back, propping himself on his side, intent on searching her eyes, checking that her answer was a serious one. Satisfied that it was, he smiled, a sparkle of triumph shining through the pleasure in his eyes. He'd won, though she'd given him enough uncertainty to want the win sealed quickly.

'I'll get the legal forms tomorrow to register our intent to marry. How quickly can you arrange our wedding, Tamalyn?'

Not a wedding.

That would feel dreadfully wrong.

'I'm willing to enter a contract of marriage with you, Fletcher. I'd prefer to do it in a registry office. I think it's the law that we have to wait a month before it can be done.'

He frowned. 'But you and your gang of friends are into weddings in a big way. Lucy was pregnant. I don't see why…'

'It's not the same,' she cut in, knowing Lucy and

Tony loved each other and had truly pledged a commitment to lifelong togetherness, as had Celine and Andrew, Kirsty and Paul. The situation between her and Fletcher was very different—a contract of marriage that guaranteed him full-time access to their child, and if the child was ordinary, he might not feel *needed*.

Not once had he ever said he loved her.

She wasn't sure he was capable of love.

And without a gifted child to keep them together…

'If it's because you think your parents wouldn't be interested in giving you a wedding…' Fletcher pressed, still frowning.

She rolled her eyes at the idea of any involvement from her parents. No way would she ask her father for anything, and if her mother knew that her daughter's husband-to-be was a billionaire, she'd stage a wedding with herself as the star. 'I won't even be telling them I'm getting married. This is strictly our business.'

'Tamalyn, I'm happy to pay for the wedding of your dreams. Anything you want.'

'No, thank you.'

He shook his head. 'Don't let pride come into this. I *want* to give you what your friends have had. *They* will want it for you. Celine will undoubtedly be outraged if I don't provide it,' he added ruefully. 'She'll go around screaming what are my billions for, and she'll be right. You should be a bride with all the trimmings.'

He was right. Her friends were not going to like her getting married in a registry office. Somehow she would have to make them understand her decision, tell them straight-out this wasn't a love-match. Partners in parenthood said it all. Hopefully they would be sympathetic to her situation and what she was making of it.

'I'll explain to my friends this isn't the right time for me,' she said dismissively.

'Because you might look more obviously pregnant in another month?' he queried, frustrated at not being able to get into her mind.

'No. Because you don't make me feel like a bride,' she said bluntly.

He grimaced in exasperation at what he obviously saw as female thinking. 'What is a bride supposed to feel like?'

'A bride should believe that her marriage will last, Fletcher.'

It gave him pause for serious thought, his eyes probing for cracks in her conviction that separation was somewhere down the track. 'What makes you think ours won't last?'

'You wanted a legal contract,' she reminded him. 'I've agreed to it. Let's go with that and see how far it works.'

His mouth twitched into a sardonic little smile. 'Still the challenging little witch.'

She returned the smile. 'Let me know when the spell wears off.'

His eyes glittered a counter-challenge. 'What if it never does?'

She arched an eyebrow. 'What did you say about the statistics of marriage?'

'I remember *you* saying there were always exceptions to the rule.'

Tammy reached out and stroked his cheek, delivering the last word, fiercely hoping that the outcome would be positive. 'Time will tell, Fletcher. Time will tell.'

He had no comeback for that.

Except to kiss her with overwhelming passion and make her feel grateful for every minute they had together...like this.

CHAPTER TWELVE

The Fourth Wedding

TAMMY thoroughly enjoyed the last gang luncheon party before Jennifer's wedding nine months later. As she drove the Lexus home to Blues Point, she smilingly reflected how much fun it had been, chatting and laughing together without the interruption of babies claiming their attention. Jennifer had declared a ban on them since she had arranged for the fitting of their bridesmaids' dresses after the luncheon and didn't want her friends distracted from the serious business of decisions on bouquets and other wedding accessories.

Celine had left her darling daughter with her mother for the day. Tony Andretti's *nonna* had claimed the right to watch over Lucy's much adored son. Tammy had had no hesitation over giving the responsibility of looking after John to Fletcher, despite the fact their son was only four months old.

He'd been a hands-on father right from the time they'd brought their baby boy home from the maternity ward. Even before that he'd obsessively devoured information about stages of her pregnancy, attended classes with her, determined on being master of the situation at the birth, and being wonderfully supportive throughout the long, painful hours of labour: sympathetic, caring, encouraging, soothing. She could not have had a better partner in parenthood.

Nor a better partner in bed.

She'd had serious doubts about how long her desirability would last for Fletcher. Amazingly he didn't seem to notice that her appearance was quite ordinary without the skilful art of a beautician and a hair stylist. Nor had he been put off by the physical changes of pregnancy, showing a fascinated pleasure in her bump and making the sex between them incredibly sensual. Sometimes she'd thought it was the child in her womb that kept her attractive to him, yet he'd been keen to resume intimacy when she'd been ready to after the birth.

For her, the chemistry was still as powerful as ever. And his love for John made him even more attractive. He was certainly capable of love. Though maybe it was only an innocent baby who could draw it from him—a baby who only knew him as the man who was there for him, building a bond that had no bad history to taint any part of it. Occasionally she felt the love overflowed to her, but not really to her as a person, more to her as the mother of his child.

She was not unhappy with Fletcher. In many ways he was a good husband. The big problem was how much he kept to himself, closeting himself in his computer room, cutting her out of anything to do with his work, which he'd set up to operate from home, and declining any invitation to join in the social activities arranged by her friends.

'I don't fit in,' was his inarguable excuse. 'I'm happy for you to go, Tamalyn. I know how much you enjoy their company.'

She did go, but it always felt wrong to her, not having Fletcher by her side when her friends had their men happily in tow. For the most part she had resigned herself to his antisocial attitude, but his refusal to attend Jennifer's and Adam's wedding was like a burr under her skin. She hadn't yet told Jennifer that he hadn't accepted the invitation. It was embarrassing, shaming, humiliating.

Having parked the Lexus in the basement garage, she headed for the elevator, thinking she had to tackle this subject again, make Fletcher understand that this was the kind of giving from him she would most appreciate. Their partnership could very well flounder if he persisted in his alien role and made no effort to find some common ground with the people she cared about.

As soon as she entered the apartment, she could hear him in the kitchen, telling John about the ingredients he was assembling for the dinner he intended to cook. It had come as a complete surprise to Tammy that he liked cooking and was very good at it, finding it a relaxing hobby from highly concentrated brain work.

'I'm home,' she called out.

'Come on round,' he called back. 'I'm getting dinner ready. I found this great new recipe on the Internet. It's baked fish—blue-eyed cod—so it won't be too heavy for you after your lunch out.'

She sighed, not wanting to dampen his ebullient mood by bringing up a bone of contention. Deciding to postpone a confrontation until tomorrow, she walked around to the galley kitchen, which was set against an internal wall with a long work-bench facing the view of the harbour. John's carry-cot was set on one end of the bench, and she checked him first, smiling over her baby's absorption in the carrot Fletcher had given him to play with.

Along the living area side of the work bench were stainless steel bar stools with designer moulded seats which turned as directed by whoever was sitting in them. Tammy hitched herself onto one, her back to the view as she watched Fletcher move to the refrigerator, take out a chilled bottle of white wine and pour them both a glass.

Be grateful for all the good things you've got with this man, she sternly told herself.

'Have a nice day?' he asked as he set the glass of wine down in front of her.

'Yes, I did, thank you.'

'Everything on track for the wedding?'

It was the wrong question. Before Tammy could monitor her mouth, a spurt of resentment escaped from it. 'Everything except you.'

Instantly his eyes were scouring hers. 'What does that mean?'

Tammy took a deep breath and made her appeal. 'I want you to be there, Fletcher. You came to the other three gang weddings. It's like…well, it's like a personal rejection not to go to Jennifer's.'

'That's absurd!' he said in arrogant dismissal. 'I had to go to Celine's. She's my sister. As for the other two, I went for you. My being there had nothing to do with your friends.'

Angry heat burned through her and spat off her tongue. 'So now that you have me tied up with a contract, you don't have to make any more effort to hold what you won from me. Is that how it is, Fletcher?'

His eyes narrowed into hard glittering slits. 'Are you saying I could lose you if I don't go?'

He didn't believe it. He didn't believe she'd walk away from what they did have together, putting their child's secure future at risk. She felt the power of his confidence crushing her will to fight. It took a tremendous effort to steel her own spirit and speak with quiet dignity. 'I'm asking you, as a favour to me…please…put yourself out for this one occasion.'

'You don't need me there, Tamalyn,' he said straight back at her with terse impatience. 'You'll be involved with the wedding party…'

'I was just as involved at the other weddings,' she argued heatedly. 'We still had time to be together.'

'It was the *only* time I could get with you,' he swiftly countered. 'That's not so anymore, is it? You'll be coming home to me. And John.'

'Don't take me for granted, Fletcher,' she warned, rising from the bar stool and moving swiftly to pick up the carry-cot. 'Cook for yourself,' she threw at him. 'I'll look after my son.'

'You only want me there as window-dressing for your friends,' he hurled after her. 'Be damned if I'll serve that superficial function! I have more productive things to do.'

She ignored him, striding on to the room they had fitted out as a nursery and shutting him out of it as fast as she could. A refrigerator and microwave oven had been installed to store and warm up bottles of formula for John. She'd had trouble with breast-feeding, generating too much milk and getting cracked nipples from pumping some of it out so the fast flow wouldn't choke John. The decision to bottle-feed had removed a lot of stress, and her baby son's contentment with the substitute lessened Tammy's sense of failure in not being able to cope with what nature had intended. She could see to John's needs tonight right here, without having to face Fletcher again.

She lifted him out of the carry-cot and sat in the rocker, needing the soothing rhythm and the comfort of cuddling her baby. Every nerve in her body was jangling. Her mind kept fretting over Fletcher's window-dressing accusation. Was it a pride thing, wanting him at the wedding? Her heart kept insisting it was more than that. People who loved each other wanted to share happy occasions, have mutual memories of them.

He didn't love her.

She'd known it all along, but tonight it hurt more than it usually did, and glossing it over with the positive aspects of their marriage didn't ease the hurt. Tears welled up and trickled down her cheeks. The silent weeping went on for a long time.

When she finally emerged from the nursery, having settled John for the night, Fletcher had obviously gone to his computer room and shut the door on her. She went to bed and woke the next morning to find him beside her but still deeply asleep. It was hours later before he made contact with her, strolling out to the balcony where she was soaking up the early-morning sunshine with John.

'Hi! Late night for me,' he said in excuse for sleeping in so long.

She nodded. Her eyes were shielded by large wrap-around sunglasses, not so much to protect them from the bright light but to hide her feelings from him. He sat on the lounger beside her, nursing a mug of coffee in his hands, looking totally relaxed and cheerful.

'I've persuaded Hans to come out to Australia,' he announced.

The German super-brain.

'Guy is coming, too.'

The American colleague.

'Max will come up to Sydney from Canberra once they're here.'

The four of them who had created the global transport network system.

'I've been playing with a new concept and we're going to put our heads together and thrash it through.'

The more productive things he had to do.

'Then I think we should start looking for a nanny,' she said.

He frowned. 'We don't need a nanny. You'll be here while I'm in conference with them.'

'I told you last night, Fletcher. Don't take me for granted. My maternity leave is almost up. I intend to ask for three days a week at the hospital.'

His mouth thinned into a vexed line. Frustration flared in his eyes.

'I have as much right to do the work I love as you have to do the work you love,' she calmly pointed out.

He couldn't manoeuvre around that argument. He'd lose if he tried and he knew it. For the sake of holding their marriage together it was truce time. But it was an uneasy truce, more like a cold war between them that Tammy was glad to escape from on the day of Jennifer's wedding.

'Enjoy yourself,' Fletcher tossed at her as she left.

'I will,' she replied, determined to do so without him.

At least she had been able to reasonably excuse his absence to Jennifer by explaining about the think-tank Fletcher had arranged with his colleagues, though she knew none of the gang really swallowed the excuse. She'd squirmed inside at the way they'd rallied around her, though she was grateful that the issue was quickly brushed aside.

Jennifer had hugged her in sympathetic support, brightly insisting, 'You'll have a better time without him if his mind is so occupied with other stuff, Tam.'

'Paul says Max is the same,' Kirsty put in, rolling her eyes. 'Off on another planet.'

Lucy struck a positive note. 'It's good that he'll be minding John, leaving you free for the whole wedding.'

'How about the two of us stay overnight at your old studio apartment, Tam,' Hannah suggested. 'We can hash over the wedding together, have us some girl fun.'

Tammy happily agreed to this arrangement. Her apartment had remained empty since she'd moved in with Fletcher, waiting for her like a security blanket so there was always somewhere for her to go if the partnership contract turned bad. Although she wasn't at the point of ending it, she didn't want to go home to Fletcher straight after the wedding as he had arrogantly assumed she would. The next day would be soon enough.

Celine was the only one who refused to gloss over the situation. 'He's a pig. He needs a smack in the face to snap him out of himself, and if I can think of a way to do it, I'll do it.'

But any anger towards Fletcher was forgotten in the excitement of the big day. In keeping with Jennifer's dream to have a fairytale wedding, she'd chosen to hold it in a castle that had been built by an eccentric millionaire over a century ago and was now an outrageously expensive function centre, not that the cost mattered because Adam was insisting on paying for it. He'd finished his second book on schedule and it was already being touted as more thrilling than his first. The castle, he'd declared, would be an interesting setting for his next book, which made everything tax deductible.

It stood majestically in a commanding position, overlooking Sydney Harbour from the old-established suburb of Hunters Hill, and the dressing for the wedding was very formal—the men in dark grey pin-striped tails, the women in splendid pastel ballgowns with big skirts, tight bodices, low scooped necklines, and off the shoulder little sleeves.

Tammy was chief bridesmaid this time, partnering Adam's brother, Jason, who was best man. Luckily, Jason proved to be amusing company. He was a graphic artist, openly gay, and like many gay men, handsome, witty and charming. He made her laugh with his comments on everything, and his best man speech was wonderful, spiced with anecdotes that had everyone rolling in their seats.

He was also a good dancer and delighted that she was, too. Dancing with him was sheer fun, no sexual tension involved. He made it easy for her to get through the wedding with a smile on her face and be genuinely happy for Jennifer and Adam.

It was only when it was all over and she was back in her old studio apartment with Hannah, hanging the creamy apricot ballgown in her clothes cupboard, that depression hit. Her other three bridesmaid dresses hung there carefully preserved in plastic bags; the mauve one from Celine's wedding, where she had first met Fletcher; the blue one from Kirsty's where she'd been unable to deny the attraction he exerted on her; the purple one from Lucy's where *he* had been unable to deny the attraction she exerted on him; now the apricot one, which marked the fact there was no happy ending in sight for her in this march of time.

It wasn't Fletcher who was trapped in a marriage by a baby. He had what he wanted. She was the one who felt caught with no way out. She could walk away from Fletcher but she couldn't walk away from her child. Nor could she take him from his father.

I'll never be a bride, she thought, closing the door on the dresses that were linked to dreams come true for her friends. Ironically, Hannah was full of her dream, too. It wasn't Jennifer's wedding she wanted to hash over with Tammy, but visions of her own.

Grant Summers, the guy she'd met at Terrigal over a year ago, was definitely getting serious about planning a future with her. Hannah was now spending most weekends with him and loving every minute of them. He owned a sports shop in the main street of the beach resort and served as a surf life-saver on Sundays, playing a leading part in the club's activities and competitions with other clubs. According to Hannah, who had always been the most sport-oriented one in the gang, he was a fantastic athlete with legions of friends.

Tammy could see the tight circle of their school gang rippling outwards, gathering more and more people who would belong to it. It made her even more sadly conscious that Fletcher chose to stand apart. If only he could learn to take an interest in others, widen his world to encompass people who had their own worth in different fields to his, they could share a much fuller life than the one contained in their private home.

Whether it was possible to draw him out she didn't know. It wasn't easy to keep fighting his rejection of what would mean a lot to her, yet she knew walking away was not a viable alternative. That struck her forcefully as she stood alone in the studio apartment after Hannah had left the next morning. It felt very empty. Her life was not here anymore. It was with John and Fletcher and she had to make the best of it.

Her resolution took a direct hit the moment she walked into their home. Fletcher was in the living room, his face darkly brooding as he stared out at the view, one hand clutching a sheaf of papers which he was slapping against his thigh. He waited until the door clicked shut then swung on her, his

eyes hard, angry, accusing, instantly throwing her
into emotional turmoil.

What had she done to deserve such an attitude
from him? She felt herself bristling at the unfair-
ness of whatever judgement he was making. He
could have been at Jennifer's wedding. He had no
right to be critical of her for any reason.

'Where have you been?'

The totally unexpected demand and the violent
feeling in his voice knocked the breath out of Tammy.
She stared at him in utter bewilderment. 'You know
where I've been. I told you I was spending the night
in my old apartment with Hannah.'

He attacked again, his eyes blazing with cynical
disbelief. 'Did you? Or was that a cover for more
illicit pleasure?'

She shook her head, unable to even guess where
he was coming from. 'What are you accusing me
of, Fletcher?'

He came at her, shaking the sheaf of papers as
though they were weapon to strike her with.
'Celine e-mailed these to me this morning.' He
flashed them at her one by one—photographs of
her laughing with Jason, dancing with Jason, very
graphically enjoying Jason's company.

Tammy instantly realised what this was about.
Celine…smacking Fletcher in the face. Celine…
stirring the pot behind Tammy's back because she

didn't approve of how her brother treated her friend. Celine…deliberately inciting jealousy and apparently succeeding.

And maybe that hadn't been a bad idea since it had put a burning burr under Fletcher's skin, goading him into demonstrating that Tammy was more important to him than she had allowed herself to think. She sent a mental thank-you to her friend and seized the chance to attack her.

'You could have been there, Fletcher, dancing with me, having fun with me. You chose not to. You waved me off, telling me to enjoy myself. Don't you think it's incredibly perverse of you now to be angry that I did?'

'Just how far did you enjoy yourself?' he snarled.

'If you'd been at the wedding, you'd know there are no grounds for this stupid suspicion.'

'Stupid?' he bit out, his eyes seething with black resentment.

'Yes, stupid!' she hit back. 'Jason Pierce is gay. Openly gay. Even you, with your habit of blanking out other people, would have seen something so obvious.'

'Gay…' His breath hissed out as though releasing some of the steam inside him. His eyes glittered with fury. 'I'm going to wring my sister's neck next time I see her.'

'The two of you do seem to have a strained relationship. Celine occasionally expresses the desire to kill you.'

'I have never attempted any interference between her and Andrew.'

'They have a marriage, Fletcher. A solid marriage that gives a lot of emotional security. That's somewhat different to a partners-in-parent-hood contract, which Celine sees as falling a long way short of being a good relationship for me.'

That visibly pulled him back from any further un-controlled outburst. He turned an intense scrutiny on her. 'Do you see it as not good enough for you?'

'Yes, I do,' she answered with point-blank honesty. 'I'd prefer to have a partner who actually wants to share in my life, what's important to me, but for John's sake, I have to learn to live with the loneliness you inflict on me every time you separate yourself from what I want to do. Every time you separate yourself to do what's important to you without telling me what it is, not letting me share in it, even if only in a limited way.'

'I didn't think complex technology would interest you,' he swiftly defended.

Her eyes flashed derision at him. 'I *can* grasp the general concept of a sophisticated transport system which was your last project. You could have tried describing your new concept instead of deciding I'm too dim for you to share it with.'

'I've never considered you dim.'

The vehement denial floated over her like an insubstantial blast of hot air. She heaved a defeated sigh. 'You just don't care enough about sharing, Fletcher. You push me away from you…' She bit her lips as she fought back a threatening rush of tears. Unsure of containing them she waved a quick dismissal of any further argument and swung away to remove herself from his presence.

'No.' He grabbed her arm, halting her.

'I want to see John,' she choked out, not looking at him.

'He's asleep.'

She struggled to free herself, desperate not to break into open weeping, pleading, 'I want to see him anyway.'

'You're doing the same thing,' he tersely accused. 'Pushing away from me.'

A mountain of anger erupted in her, blasting away the tears of weakness, giving her the strength to tear her arm out of his dominating grasp. He wasn't taking in anything she'd said, wasn't about to change his behaviour to make their relationship better. Not only had he virtually accused her of infidelity because he'd scorned being a guest at Jennifer's wedding, he was twisting her argument around to lay fault at her door rather than look at what he'd been doing himself.

'The only reason I'm here is because my son is here,' she hurled at him with venomous ferocity. 'And you know what I hope, Fletcher? I hope he doesn't have one skerrick of your child-prodigy genetic pattern, because if that proves to be the case, I hope you'll lose interest in him and leave him to me. And I'll teach him that everyone has value and not to arbitrarily dismiss them because they're not the same as him. I'll teach him to be a caring human being. I'll even teach him to try to understand his father who never learnt those lessons.'

It wasn't a smack in the face that was of no real account this time. It was a hard hit, striking at the basis of their contract, and it gave Tammy vicious satisfaction to see the draining of his arrogant confidence, the blank shock in his eyes, the loss of colour in his face, the frozen look that told her his brilliant mind was jammed for once.

She marched off to the nursery.

John was asleep, lying peacefully in his cot, unaware of the war being waged between his parents. He was only four months old—too soon to tell if he was unusually gifted.

Let him be mine, Tammy begged whatever Fate had worked so malevolently to make her pregnant in the first place. Surely this one kindness could be granted to her.

Please...let him be mine!

CHAPTER THIRTEEN

FLETCHER withdrew from her.

He made no reference to her criticism of their relationship. Over the next few weeks their only conversation was about household arrangements. They lived in the same space, ate meals together, slept in the same bed, but he'd wrapped an impenetrable wall around himself that made him untouchable. Even caring for their son was separated into mutually exclusive areas.

They didn't employ a nanny. Tammy dropped that idea, feeling that neither of them could bear the intrusion of another person in their tension-ridden world. Fletcher looked after John while she worked her three days at the hospital. She had full custody of him when Fletcher met up with his colleagues at an apartment Hans was renting on the other side of the harbour. At other times they were careful to share their son on a fairly equal basis, both of them adopting the truce-like state of polite consideration.

As one miserable week followed another, Tammy deeply regretted having thrown such a comprehensive rejection at Fletcher. He was not a bad person. And saying she didn't want their child to be like him was a very nasty blow below the belt, implying she'd hate the situation if he was and that wasn't true. She'd work hard at providing John with a happier childhood than Fletcher had known.

As soon as their son was settled for the night, Fletcher went to his computer room, and during those lonely hours before she went to sleep alone, Tammy thought a lot about what he'd told her about his life. She wondered if his arrogance was actually a coat of protective armour, a denial that anything or anyone could hurt him. Their intimacy throughout her pregnancy had probably made him feel secure about giving what he did of himself to her, but giving anything of himself to others on a more casual basis...that was territory he didn't want to occupy. It opened him up to responses he preferred not to deal with.

The man with the super-brain...the man with more money than most people could get their heads around...a dazzling man who wasn't quite human like everyone else...except he was.

Human enough to want her so much he'd been unable to stop himself from pursuing her...human enough to love their child without reservation…human enough to erupt with violent feeling when he thought his trust in her had been betrayed… human enough to be so deeply wounded by her not wanting their son to be like his father that he'd retreated back inside himself, disconnecting from her as much as was possible without contravening the terms of their contract.

She missed what they had shared together.

She wished she had given more consideration, more understanding, to why he chose to let her go off alone to social activities instead of resenting his refusal to window-dress a private contract that was no one else's business.

She wanted him to want her again.

The huge problem was—how to reverse what seemed irreversible.

Jennifer and Adam returned from their honeymoon. They'd spent three weeks touring Africa and Egypt and Jennifer had video footage she wanted to show and a heap of gifts for the gang. Instead of their monthly luncheon in Sydney, she suggested they all come up to the Blue Mountains for the weekend, bringing their men and babies with them, have a long, late lunch with her and Adam at his Leura cottage on the Saturday afternoon, stay at the famous Carrington Hotel at Katoomba overnight and do whatever they liked on Sunday before going home.

Everyone loved the idea.

'Tell Fletcher he can go trekking into the Jamieson Valley,' Jennifer advised Tammy. 'That might get him to come. You said you climbed the mountain on Lord Howe.'

'Yes, we did. But if I end up coming alone, don't make a big thing of it. Okay?'

'Okay. But you must come, Tam. We'd all miss you if you didn't.'

For the first time in her long friendship with the gang, Tammy didn't want to attend this get-together. Making arrangements to go would necessitate speaking to Fletcher about it, bringing up a painful reminder of the rift between them—the cause of it on her side. Not that it would make any difference to what had become entrenched alienation on his part, she told herself, yet she still shied from taking another step away from him.

It threw her into confusion when he brought up the subject. She'd come home from an eight-hour shift at the hospital. Fletcher had cooked a very tasty spaghetti marinara for dinner and she'd gratefully complimented him on it.

'Your monthly luncheon must be coming up,' he remarked matter-of-factly. 'Where's the venue this time?'

'I don't think I'll go,' she muttered, dropping her gaze to the glass of Chardonnay he'd poured for her, picking it up and idly swirling the wine around.

'Why not?'

She grimaced at what had to be perverse curiosity in something that didn't interest him. 'Jennifer wants to make it a weekend affair,' she answered reluctantly.

'Not just a luncheon for the six of you?'

'No.' She recited the whole plan to get the issue over and done with, then concentrated on sipping the Chardonnay to remove the dryness from her mouth.

'Have they all agreed to it?' Fletcher asked, as though he was assessing the situation.

Tammy looked directly at him, not understanding why he was persisting with these questions. 'Yes. They're making the long lunch at Adam's a joint effort. Tony is taking a case of fine wines. Kirsty and Paul are providing a platter of King Island cheeses. Hannah and Grant will be bringing an esky of fresh prawns from Terrigal. Celine and Andrew are doing salads. Adam and Jennifer will have the meat for the barbecue. They're all looking forward to it.'

'What are we marked down to provide?'

We?

A wild hope kicked into Tammy's heart as she stared at him, seeing no hint of mockery in his eyes, more a steady flame of purpose which was not about to be derailed.

'I didn't hear any sweets in that list of food,' he

ran on musingly. 'Something light with fruit would probably be best…caramelised pears…maybe simply oranges and kiwi fruit soaked in cointreau… a palate-cleanser….'

Tammy was supposed to take fancy breads. She had thought of paying to have them delivered by a bakery, but the possibility that Fletcher was actually thinking of contributing…of accompanying her…kept her mouth firmly shut. If cooking something—preparing something—made it easier for him to join in with her friends, no way was she going to mention anything that might put him off.

Having rambled through several choices for sweets, Fletcher asked, 'What do you think they'd like? What would be most welcome?'

She'd barely listened, could barely catch enough breath to speak. 'You, Fletcher,' she blurted out. 'You would be most welcome.'

Her heart caromed around her chest.

Had that sounded too much like a demand?

Her eyes begged him to take this step towards her. She needed him with her, needed to know he cared about their relationship, needed *him* to know she wanted him in her life.

'Oh, I doubt that,' he drawled sardonically. 'I expect they'll all want to cut me down to size.'

'Not if you focus on them,' she pressed. 'Ask Adam about his books. Bring up money markets for Paul and Andrew to get their teeth into. You like wine. Get Tony's advice on the best vintages. And Grant is into physical challenges. Chat to him about diving, climbing…. It's just a matter of moving onto ground that they're comfortable with. If you show you want to enjoy their company, they'll enjoy yours. They're good people, Fletcher. If you'll just give them a chance….'

He nodded, a wry little smile lurking on his lips, a strange, unreadable glitter in his eyes. 'Call Jennifer and tell her we're both coming.' He rose from his chair. 'I'll go and look up sweets recipes on the Internet, find something special. It will be our contribution to the party.'

'Thank you,' she breathed, too overwhelmed with relief and gratitude to make any move herself.

She sat at the dining-table, watching him walk away, every nerve in her body buzzing with the thrill of realisation that he was giving *them* a chance to make a future together. He'd decided to fight her rejection, attack the reasons behind it, and a huge swell of love for him rolled through her. She resolved not to be critical of how he behaved with her friends, to help him as much as she could, to do everything in her power to draw him out of his sense of isolation.

Jennifer was delighted with the news.

She obviously spread it to the gang very quickly

because not half an hour later Celine called Tammy, sounding smugly pleased with herself. 'So, he's not going to let you out to party alone again.'

'It's not like that, Celine,' she quickly insisted.

'Oh, come on, Tam. He needed a shake-up. Sending those photos did the trick.'

'No. It damaged us, Celine,' she said seriously, needing her friend to revise her attitude towards her brother. 'I know you meant well, but… I don't think you understand Fletcher. His life has been very different to yours, not so easy in any social sense. Even in your family he felt like a cuckoo in your nest, not belonging. What you see as arrogance…it's shutting off the rejection he feels coming from most people because he's not like them. He was born different. Have you ever thought about how it was for him…being different…envying you because you were normal?'

'Envying me?' She sounded so incredulous, it had obviously never occurred to her that her super-brain brother could feel anything but superior, floating loftily over everyone else.

'Please don't take any snide cracks at him when we meet up at Jennifer's party,' Tammy pleaded. 'If you'd try to make him feel welcome, I'd really appreciate it, Celine.'

'Okay,' she agreed without much conviction. 'If that will help. I didn't mean to cause damage, Tam.

I thought… I'm sorry… I promise to stay right out of your relationship in future. You clearly know my brother better than I do.' She hesitated a moment then anxiously asked, 'Should I apologise to him over the photos?'

'It might do some good…if there's an appropriate moment. Don't make a big thing of it,' Tammy quickly advised.

'Right! I'll wait and watch and choose my moment. And thanks for opening up to me, Tam. I can see I need to re-think quite a few things.'

'You and Fletcher are brother and sister. I'd like it if you could be friends, too, Celine.'

'I'll really make an effort,' her friend promised.

Tammy came home from work the next evening to another surprise. Fletcher told her that his mother had telephoned, saying she was looking after Celine's daughter for the Saturday and the Sunday of the Blue Mountains trip and would love to look after John, as well, arguing she hadn't seen much of her grandson and it would be good for him and Tammy to have some free time together.

Celine at work behind the scenes, Tammy instantly thought. 'What did you say?' she asked warily.

'I said I'd have to consult with you,' he replied, a hard challenge in his eyes.

It meant they would be alone together in the hotel

room, without their child as a buffer between them—
the child whom Tammy had so bitingly stated was
the only reason she was staying with Fletcher.

A self-conscious flush heated her cheeks.
Agreeing to the plan would mean she wanted the
more-intimate situation. If he still turned away
from her when the time came... But the risk of
being torn up emotionally had to be taken if this
rift was ever to be bridged. He hadn't rejected his
mother's plan outright. Maybe this was his way of
reaching out to her.

She forced a smile. 'I think it's nice that your
mother wants to have John. Mine would hate
owning up to having a grandson.'

'You're happy to go along with the arrangement?'
he bored in, not prepared to assume anything.

'Yes,' she said quickly, then in a moment of
stomach-roiling panic, added, 'If you are.'

He nodded, his eyelashes lowering, but not
before Tammy glimpsed a dark blaze of satisfaction. 'I'll let her know we're both fine with it,' he
said in a flat tone, apparently intent on waiting to
see how well the party with her friends went before
committing himself to any further attempts at
sharing her life.

Tammy liked Celine's parents. It was relatively
easy to remain relaxed with them during their brief
visit to pick up John on the designated day, but as

soon as they were gone, tension started mounting in her so badly, she dreaded the drive up to Leura with Fletcher. They loaded up the Lexus with their overnight bags, the fancy breads she'd bought, and the selection of sweets Fletcher had decided was better than just one choice. Once in the car and on their way, they didn't talk at all. Fletcher played a selection of music, which was some relief because negotiating any conversation with him seemed perilous at this point.

Everyone arrived at Adam's cottage more or less at the same time. The business of taking in their provisions for the party covered any awkwardness over greetings. Grant, whom Fletcher didn't know, immediately went into a friendly 'Hail fellow, well met,' routine, clapping him on the back, smiling broadly as he said Hannah had told him Fletcher shared his passion for meeting the challenge of untamed nature, and suggesting the four of them do a trek tomorrow morning, taking on the famous rock formations of the Three Sisters at Katoomba.

'Are you up for it, Tamalyn?' Fletcher asked as though he was interested in the offer.

'I am if you are,' she answered.

'Deal!' he said, grinning at Grant, and Tammy started to relax.

Jennifer was effusively welcoming, especially when she eyed over the sweets Fletcher had brought. 'Wow! This is a dream. A man who cooks delectable desserts!'

'I'm only good for erotic stuff like oysters in the shell,' Adam drily commented.

'Having read and been very engaged by your first book, I don't think you're limited to oysters in the field of erotica,' Fletcher remarked, making everyone laugh and toss excerpts from the book at Adam, showing appreciation of his wicked imagination.

It set a happy mood for the party and Tammy relaxed enough to enjoy the company of her friends.

The weather was kind to them. It was a lovely mild sunny afternoon, no mist obscuring the view of the Jamieson Valley—the blue haze of its massed eucalypt trees and the stark cliffs of the mountains strikingly beautiful. They sat outside, feasting at a long tressle table loaded with fine food and wine, chatting companionably on many topics. The only time Tammy's stomach clenched with concern was when Paul brought up Fletcher's work.

'Max tells me you're spearheading a new project. He visited Kirsty and me when he was in Sydney, meeting up with you and your other colleagues,' he said with an air of keen curiosity. 'No sitting on your laurels, Fletcher?'

'I've never actually worked for laurels,' Fletcher answered with a shrug. 'It's more the fascination of the challenge, beating the problems. The laurels are a by-product I'm not particularly comfortable with.'

There were a few moments of silence following this quiet declaration—whether from the shock of it or simply a pause for consideration Tammy couldn't tell. She fiercely hoped no-one would say they could live very comfortably with a few billions.

Thankfully, no-one did.

'So what is it you're working on this time?' Paul pushed. 'Max wouldn't say since the concept is yours.'

It put Fletcher right in the spotlight, everyone looking at him expectantly, and Tammy held her breath, hoping he wouldn't freeze them out. They were simply interested, not viewing him as a tall poppy they wanted to cut down.

Fletcher shook his head, a wry little smile twitching his lips. 'I'm no longer interested in creating some global change in technology. Having John has made me want to make things better for children. It struck me that computer games can be very powerful tools for teaching skills that will be useful to them, an easier path to learning if the learning is subtly mixed with entertainment. Maths is a mystery to a lot of children, but it needn't be if the basic principles are packaged in a way they absorb while playing a game.'

'Do you mean maths would become a more natural tool to them if they were drawn into it by the computer games?' Andrew asked.

Fletcher nodded. 'That's what we're aiming for.'

'Well I think it's marvellous!' Celine said, looking admiringly at her brother.

'Me, too,' Lucy chimed in enthusiastically. 'We'll certainly be buying these games for our children when they're done, won't we, Tony?'

'Absolutely. It's a numbers business, running a vineyard,' he backed up, smiling adoringly at his wife.

Tammy wished Fletcher would smile at her like that, but the fact that he'd opened up about his work to her friends did give her a brilliant burst of happiness.

'Come to think of it,' Adam mused, 'the more skilled we are at maths, the better everything works. As a writer, you can't really nail a story unless it has a stringent inner logic. And when you're surfing, Grant, you must need precision timing for riding a wave to get the optimum surge.'

'You're always assessing percentages,' Grant agreed.

'It's a must for banking,' Paul put in.

'And accountancy,' Andrew added.

'One way or another, we all have to juggle numbers,' Kirsty said, smiling at Fletcher. 'I hope

you and your gang can beat all the problems wit
this project and get it out there for the kids.'

'Let's drink to that,' Tony said, rising to osten
tatiously open another bottle. 'Now, this wine i
from a particularly good vintage….'

The rest of the afternoon drifted by very pleas
antly. After they had completely stuffed themselve
with delicious food and drank most of Tony's fin
wines, they all trooped into Adam's living room t
watch a highly edited video of the honeymoon i
Africa and Egypt, Adam giving an amusing com
mentary and Jennifer handing out gifts they'
bought at the places featured.

Considering the probability they were all ove
the alcohol limit for driving, they decided to leav
their cars at the cottage until tomorrow and tak
taxis to the hotel. Tammy and Fletcher shared on
with Hannah and Grant, all of them still in an ebul
lient mood from the party and making plans fo
their walk in the morning. It wasn't until th
couples parted to go to their rooms at the hotel tha
Tammy started feeling edgy again.

Instantly the silence between them gathered
thick sense of constraint. There was no touching
Fletcher carried their bags. Tammy nursed the doo
key in her hands. By the time they reached thei
room, her mind was hopelessly stressed wit
sorting through the past few hours for assurance

hat Fletcher had really enjoyed himself in the ompany of her friends. Or had he merely pretended to for the sake of appearing congenial? If he latter, pretence wouldn't stand up for long and hey'd end up living under the same roof but eading separate lives.

She opened the door, stepped inside the room, vaited until Fletcher had moved in with the bags, hen closed it behind them, acutely aware that the kind of future relationship they would have was ery much at stake. Anxiety had her bursting into peech even before he'd set their bags on the uggage rack provided.

'Was it all right for you?'

He dumped the bags and turned to her.

Her hands flew out in agitated appeal as she babbled on. 'I mean the party. I thought you fitted n very well, not apart from it at all, but that's not he point, is it? It's whether you had a good time, vhether you felt any pleasure in their company, nough for you to find it a positive experience ather than a…a…'

'A barely tolerable one?' he supplied with a quizical lift of one eyebrow.

Her throat seized up, unable to emit a word, her yes begging for an answer that would ease the ituation between them.

He started walking back towards her, speaking

in a rueful tone. 'I was wrong and you were right, Tamalyn. They are likeable people. I didn't sense any envy. There was no spite, no sneaking ambition to use me for their own profit. I think Paul has a problem with having Max as his brother, just as Celine has a problem with me. The difference is too close for them to be comfortable with it.'

She swallowed hard and pleaded, 'But Paul did show respect for you, and Celine admired what you've set out to do for children.'

'True.' His mouth twitched in amusement. 'She even took me aside to apologise for meddling with the photos from Jennifer's wedding, explaining she'd been angry on your behalf because she'd thought I'd let you down by not going, but she was very glad that I'd climbed down from my pinnacle and come to the party with you, so I'm now forgiven for past slights.'

Tammy rolled her eyes in exasperation. That was *so* Celine.

Fletcher laughed. 'It's impossible to change years of habit in one day, Tamalyn.'

'But you tried giving out more of yourself, Fletcher, and I thought you got a good response.'

'Yes. I must admit I was surprised, pleased and gratified that the work I put into the party was well received.' He halted directly in front of her and she felt the force of his dynamic energy encompassing her, powering through her nervous system, making er body feel tremulously on the edge of being drawn irresistibly to his. 'The only question now is…' His eyes engaged hers with heart-stopping intensity as he lifted a hand and gently, seductively, stroked the outline of her mouth with a light, teasing finger. '…do I get a reward for my efforts?'

Reward?

The word echoed through her mind, setting off a wild melee of desires that had been suppressed for far too long. It was utterly impossible for her mouth to repeat it. Her lips were tingling with mesmerised pleasure. Tension exploded into action. Her arms lifted and flung themselves around his neck, her body springing against his in a rush of reckless need.

He wrapped her in a fierce embrace and kissed her as though he wanted to draw everything she was into himself, owning her so totally she'd be incapable of choosing to part from him.

With her own feelings running so high, Tammy returned the intensity of his passion, revelling in his need for her, wanting to deepen it so far he could never be free of it.

They moved to the bed in an almost blind flurry of urgency, whipping off their clothes, reaching wildly for each other, seizing, hands scrambling over flesh and muscle, bodies grinding in a frenzy of craving, mouths and tongues in deep entanglement as they fell on the bed, Tammy's legs closing around him like a vise as Fletcher speared his body into hers, lifting her to take all of him.

It was a mindless time of intense feeling, wave after wave of sensation storming through her, pushing her relentlessly to the ultimate peak of ecstacy, and such a sweet meltdown afterwards with Fletcher holding her close, maintaining the euphoric intimacy, their hearts pounding in unison. She didn't want to think, didn't want to speak, just wanted to stay nestled warmly in the moment.

It was Fletcher who broke the peaceful idyll, rolling her gently onto her back, kissing her forehead, smiling into her eyes. 'Tell me it's not just our child keeping you with me, Tamalyn.'

'Okay. You get to me, too,' she conceded. Feeling much more confident now that they might make a good future together, she teasingly added, 'I think I like the reward system.'

'Ah…the challenging witch is back.' He sounded pleased.

She cocked an eyebrow at him. 'Does that work for you?'

He laughed. 'Let's say it gets to me.'

'Then we're both in the same boat.'

'I'll try to make sharing it better.'

She smiled.

He kissed her.

And Tammy felt a lot better about everything.

CHAPTER FOURTEEN

The Fifth Wedding

HANNAH arranged for a beautician to come and spray them all with fake tan so they would look right for the beach wedding. They painted their fingernails and toenails a perfect shell pink to match their dresses, which were strapless and draped in a sarong style. They would be barefoot for the ceremony on the sand but they had pink sandals to put on afterwards. Their bouquets were made of pink and cream frangipanis and they were wearing a circle of the same flowers in their hair. Tammy's long locks had been swept to one side and softly rolled forward over one shoulder—Tahitian style, Hannah had declared.

Having another gang wedding was wonderfully exciting, though for Tammy the excitement had the additional delight of Fletcher's willingly active involvement on the groom's side. Over the past six months he'd loosened up quite a lot with her friends and found Grant especially companionable. Both men shared a deep appreciation of nature, had very athletic physiques, and enjoyed testing their strength and agility on difficult climbs and bush-walks. The sea was also very much their playground and the two couples had spent several weekends doing various activities together. It had pleased Tammy enormously when Grant had asked Fletcher to be one of his groomsmen and there had been no hesitation in his acceptance of the role.

To make everything perfect, it was a beautiful day—bright and sunny with a cloudless blue sky. Everyone was bubbling with high spirits as they were finally driven down to Terrigal Esplanade, the white limousines heralding the arrival of the bridal party. The resort town was abuzz with people, pavement cafés crowded with patrons, the picnic tables under the Norfolk Pines that lined the beachfront occupied by families, the beach itself a kaleidoscope of colour with sun umbrellas, bright towels, deckchairs and masses of people in their swimming gear.

Grant Summers' wedding was a big event in this local community, drawing a horde of spectators. A long hessian mat had been rolled out from the front of the Surf Club, down the central ramp to the beach, along the sand to the huge, open-sided marquee which was shading the wedding guests,

forming an aisle right to where the marriage celebrant and the groom and his attendants were
waiting. Life-savers in their club colours were lined
up on either side of it between the ramp and the
marquee. 'Here Comes the Bride' blared out from
the club's loudspeakers, and the spectators broke
into wild applause as Tammy led off the procession.

Which she'd also done at Celine's wedding
when Fletcher had been designated her partner—
their very first meeting. Today he was the fifth
groomsman again and Tammy had an eerie sense
of déjà vu as she paced herself along the mat to the
marquee, her gaze skating down the line of men
waiting beside Grant.

The picture was different. The men were not
wearing formal black suits. Their attire was
smart/casual; white slacks, white jacket, open-
necked pink shirt. But the impact of seeing Fletcher
was the same, so commandingly handsome the
others faded into insignificance, and her heart beat
faster at the knowledge he was hers, not just for
today, but her partner for a long, long time to come,
given that John was barely a toddler.

Just as he had at their first sight of each other
almost two years ago, he dazzled her with his smile.

Tammy smiled back.

Did he still see her as exotic—a black-haired
witch who held him spellbound?

She hoped so, needing to feel forever wanted by him.

All five bridesmaids completed their line-up on the bride's side. Hannah faced the celebrant with Grant. The ceremony began, the vows of a true marriage being solemnly recited. Tammy's mind drifted to her own stark contract with Fletcher—terms agreed to because of their child.

John was ten months old now, once again being looked after by Fletcher's parents today, along with Celine's daughter, Samantha. The two grandchildren liked each other's company though they were as different as chalk and cheese. Samantha was like a gorgeous little doll, very placid and easy to please. John was a very active livewire. He'd started picking up words at seven months, was walking at nine months, and he organised games around Samantha who sat in the middle of them, adoring his attention.

There was no doubt John was extremely forward for his age, and sometimes Tammy thought she saw a look of recognition pass between father and son as though they knew their minds shared the same patterns. But it was Mummy John wanted when he was upset about anything, so she didn't feel cut out by their special bond. She suspected there would be difficult times ahead for their child, so it had definitely been the right decision to live with Fletcher, not only for John's sake, but for her own as well.

They'd come a long way since Celine's wedding. The connection between them had been there from the beginning, yet it had been frayed by so many conflicts, holding on to it had not been easy. Tammy felt more secure with it now. Probably not as secure as her friends felt with their husbands who openly loved them, but she knew there would never be any other man for her, so what she had with Fletcher was good enough.

Grant and Hannah were declared man and wife. The marriage certificate was signed. The photographer shepherded the bridal party down to the edge of the surf for some action shots, kicking through the dying waves, Grant twirling his bride over them. The men had to roll up their trouser legs so as not to get them wet and Tammy watched Fletcher do it, admiring the strong muscles of his calves. As he straightened up, he caught her gaze on him and grinned at her.

It was like a sledgehammer hitting her heart. He was still drop-dead gorgeous, still had the sexual magnetism that shot out an electric charge, sending a rush of tingles through her entire body. He walked over to where she stood with her friends, waiting to perform as Hannah's bridesmaids for the photographer. He held out his hand to her, a sexy simmer in his brilliant dark eyes.

'We could show them how to dance on the sand.'

She laughed, shaking her head. 'It's not our time to shine today. We're here to complement the starring couple.'

He wrapped his hand around hers, squeezing it possessively. 'I want you to have your day to shine, Tamalyn, and sooner or later I'll make it happen.'

'Oh? What is that supposed to mean?' she queried, surprised by the intensity of purpose in his voice.

He gave her a quirky little smile. 'It means I'm going to have my way with you, and I'll start by dancing you off your feet after the official wedding program ends and the party starts.'

She gave him an arch look. 'I seem to remember you had that attitude at your sister's wedding.'

'Ah, but I didn't know what I was dealing with then.'

'And you do now?'

'Intimately,' he declared with his old arrogant confidence.

She heaved a mock sigh. 'I preferred being challenging.'

He laughed. 'Believe me, I'm acutely aware of how challenging you still are, but I'm determined on winning in the end.'

The photographer called out for them to oblige

him with some action poses and Tammy was left mystified by what Fletcher wanted to win in the end. She wondered about it as they mixed with the others but there was virtually no chance to pursue the question privately. The gang was intent on having fun and swept Tammy and Fletcher along with them.

It wasn't until the bridal waltz—many hours later—that they were alone together again and Tammy was happy simply to be dancing with Fletcher. The big reception room which stretched along the top floor of the Surf Club had a large dance floor—room enough to twirl around and indulge in fancy steps with a masterful partner who took as much sensual pleasure in every move as she did.

The official waltz was followed by many other dances—the DJ pumping out one music track after another. After leading her through a particularly wicked cha-cha which left them both panting with excitement, Fletcher curled a protective arm around her waist and negotiated their way through the crowd towards one of the arches that led to the balcony overlooking the beach.

They reached the balcony wall and he hugged her closer to him as they stood enjoying the refreshing coolness of the salt-tanged breeze from the ocean. Neither of them spoke, content with the intimacy of their togetherness. After a while

Fletcher rubbed his cheek against the silky fall of her hair and murmured, 'Happy?'

'Yes,' she answered on a heartfelt sigh.

'Happy with me?'

She turned to him with a smile. 'You know I am.'

His eyes glittered with the intensity of purpose she had felt coming from him when they'd been on the beach. 'Happy enough to be my bride, Tamalyn?'

'Your bride?' she queried, not understanding what was in his mind.

He drew her into his embrace and his voice was furred with deep emotion as he explained. 'We're legally married but I know you didn't enter into our contract with a happy heart. You didn't feel right about where we were then, so you wouldn't have a wedding. Listening to Hannah and Grant today, making their vows to love and cherish each other for the rest of their lives, I understood what you felt. You didn't believe I loved and cherished you. And in all honesty, I can't say I did at that point.'

Did he now?

If eyes were the windows to one's soul, his were too dark for her to see that far, but she fiercely hoped he was leading her there.

'It was like I had to have you. Right from our first meeting you incited that compulsion and, as much as I tried to dismiss it, nothing I did or said to myself would make it go away. And the hell of it was, I couldn't fit you into any frame I was familiar with, couldn't nail you down because you wouldn't be nailed. Once the initial shock of your pregnancy wore off, I was actually elated by it because it gave me the power to get what I wanted—you and our child.'

She understood the compulsion. It had driven her, too, completely beyond the dictates of any normal common sense. Was it some primal instinct insisting this is the man…this is the woman? A chemistry that neither of them could control? Or was it one soul calling to another, ignoring the barriers of different life experiences, recognising only that they fitted together, if the fit could be found?

Maybe it was all of those things.

The only certainty Tammy had was she loved this man—for better or for worse—and she longed to hear…

'But you must know I do love you, Tamalyn,' he said, as though his mind was tuned into hers. 'Very deeply,' he fervently assured her. 'And I cherish the person you are, all you've given me of yourself, drawing me into appreciating a world of people who didn't deserve a cynical dismissal. You've made me see things very differently.'

He reached up and stroked her cheek with featherlight fingers, giving her the sense of being so precious he was awed by her. 'Most of all I see you, Tamalyn. Not just as the most desirable woman I could ever have in my bed, but the woman who makes my life worth living, the woman I love having as the mother of my child…the woman I love for everything she is. I can say that vow— "forsaking all others"—with complete sincerity, because for me there is only you.'

Her heart overflowed with happiness. A huge welling of emotion pushed tears into her eyes. She'd waited so long to hear this from him, hoping for it but never sure it would come. 'I love you, too,' she confided without hesitation, her arms winding around his waist, hugging him tightly as she buried her face against the strong warm column of his throat and spilled out more of her feelings. 'You've been the only man for me ever since we met. The night of Kirsty's wedding, I wanted you to be my first lover, my only lover, Fletcher. And when we were on Lord Howe I thought you loved me, but you only wanted to use me then.'

'No.' His hand threaded through her hair and gently cupped the back of her head. She felt his voice rumbling from his throat as he explained further. 'Not "use," Tamalyn. I wanted to keep you with me, and I thought the power of my wealth was enough to do it. Even as I was acquiring the apartment and the car before proposing marriage to you, I was still thinking it. But I know now it never was enough, never would be. I had to change my views and you were the force that changed them. I don't think I knew what love was then. I only knew I couldn't bear to lose you.'

'It doesn't matter any more,' she murmured. The past was behind them. They were here in this wonderful moment.

'To me, it does. I robbed you of a dream by manipulating you into marriage. All your friends have had their weddings—their day to shine as a bride—and I want to give you that, Tamalyn, make everything right for you. The vows Hannah and Grant exchanged today—they're real to us now, aren't they? You can believe I mean every word?'

'Yes,' she said in giddy joy.

'Then let me give you a wedding with all the trimmings. I want you to have our love for each other openly celebrated in front of your friends. I want you to feel like my bride, be my bride, and have it as a happy memory for the rest of our lives.'

He tilted her head back, wanting to see acceptance in her eyes, and she saw in his the determination to win it…getting his own way with her in the end. But it was a beautiful way, a loving way, and she happily gave in to him.

'I'd like that very much, Fletcher.'

His face lit with joyful triumph. 'Leave it to me, Tamalyn. I'll make it right for you. You just dream up whatever you'd like and that's what we'll have.'

'It's your wedding, too.'

'I want what you want. Though right now I feel like dancing the night away. Are you with me?'

She laughed. 'Lead the way.'

He did and she went with him, feeling the future stretching out in front of them—the kind of future that made her want to dance, too—dance with twinkling toes and bubbles of joy and stars in her eyes because Fletcher loved her and wanted to celebrate their love for each other in a wedding that promised a lifetime of commitment.

Not for their child.

For them.

CHAPTER FIFTEEN

One Year Later
Lord Howe Island
The Sixth Wedding

FORTUNATELY the property where Tammy and Fletcher had stayed last time had six boutique apartments, accommodation for the whole gang, which made for a great time together leading up to the wedding. The rest of the guests were all over the place. Fletcher had virtually booked every available room on the island, paying for them well in advance, organising the flights in and out, ensuring that no-one would miss out on the celebration of their marriage. The man was an absolute powerhouse when he put his mind to something, making Tammy feel she was the luckiest woman in the world to have him.

And here it was at last—their wedding day.

She couldn't stop smiling as her friends fussed around her, getting ready for the ceremony. They'd

swarmed into her and Fletcher's apartment as soo
as he'd left it this morning, taking John with hir
to the apartment designated for the men to ge
ready. Her friends were happy for her. She wa
happy for herself.

'I didn't think this wedding would happer
and I'm so glad it is,' Celine said, grinning fror
ear to ear.

'In great style, too!' Kirsty said in warr
approval. 'I must say I like the way he's spendin;
up big to give you the best day he can, Tam. Show
how much he loves you.'

Tammy smiled. 'He's spending far more on .
project that's very dear to my heart.'

'You mean the computer games for children?
Lucy asked, keen on anything that might benefi
them. She and Tony wanted a big family and they'
had another baby a few months ago.

'No. They're not ready for marketing yet,
Tammy answered. 'This is something *I* wished wa
available. We're going to build a centre that will hel;
distressed mothers who can't cope with their nev
babies. I've seen this problem so many times anc
couldn't do enough about it to really help. Fletcher'
already got people looking for the right property.'

'Wow! That's great, Tam. And so are *you*,
Jennifer said, looking proud of her. 'You've really
found your Mr Right.'

Celine shook her head incredulously. 'I would never have believed my brother would turn into a humanitarian. That's convinced me. He really loves you, Tammy.'

Hannah pounced, wanting her curiosity satisfied. 'I know you chose to have the wedding here because this is where the two of you really got down to basics, but are you zipping off somewhere else for a honeymoon?'

'No, just a few more days here, then we're going home.'

Hannah looked disappointed. 'Well, I guess this is romantic enough.'

Tammy hesitated a moment, wondering how her friends would react, but it was going to happen anyway. 'Actually we do have something planned, but we have to wait a while to do it. Fletcher has booked us on a trip to outer space, a once-in-a-lifetime experience. One of the guys who created Google is doing it, too.'

Their jaws dropped in unison.

Celine recovered first. 'Outer space. That is so *him*. Do you actually want to go on a spaceship, Tammy?'

'Yes. I think it will be marvellous. Seeing the earth from way up there, the moon, the stars, the whole universe spread around us…. I can't imagine anything more fabulous.'

'Now I know you're right for each other. Mad... both of you.'

'Oh, Celine, you're so *grounded,*' Jennifer chided. 'I think it's wonderful, Tammy taking off to the stars. Who'd have thought any of us would ever have the chance?'

'Yes. You go for it, girl!' Hannah enthusiastically approved, instantly applying their old catch-cry.

'Just imagine!' Lucy trilled in delight. 'I'll be able to take my kids outside one night, point up to the sky and tell them *my* friend is up there in a spaceship.'

'*Our* friend,' Kirsty corrected her. 'We'll be so proud of you, Tam. Well, we are anyway. And we're so glad you finally got to be the bride.'

'Who's going to be late for the ceremony if we don't get a move on,' Celine warned. She smiled at Tammy. 'I'm one up on the rest of the gang. I can say my sister-in-law is flying in outer space. And my brother took her there. I won't even mention you're both in the grip of lunar madness.'

They all laughed at her good-humoured concession, then happily settled back into getting ready. Tammy loved the silk chiffon dresses she'd had made for her friends. The halter-necked crossover bodice was red with a red tie at the waist, but the skirt was a lovely flowing concoction of graduated lengths in red and orange and yellow, like the gorgeous hibiscus flowers that grew on the island, a few of which comprised their bouquets.

Her gown was in a figure-hugging mermaid style and made of white silk satin. Lace and pearl beading artfully decorated the strapless bodice. Three diagonal rows of lace and beading ran around her waist, hips and thighs, and from knee length the skirt flared out with lace and beading around the hem. Her veil was attached to a pearl tiara, and when she was fully dressed, the gang gathered around, beaming satisfaction in the full effect of the bridal party and telling Tammy she looked breathtakingly beautiful.

I'm the bride, she thought, her heart swelling with happiness as she stared at her reflection in the mirror. *The last one. But the best wedding of all because it's me and I'm Fletcher's bride.*

A mini-bus took them down to Ned's Beach where all the guests had gathered at the perfectly manicured green park above the cleanest beach in the world. Fletcher's mother and Lucy's mother—both of them longtime friends—had the three children lined up waiting for them: Samantha as flower-girl, carrying a basket of rose-petals; Lucy's son, Mario, and John flanking her as page-boys.

This was the ultimate gang wedding, Tammy thought, thrilled that it had turned out this way

with her friends as bridesmaids, their husbands a.
groomsmen and the children taking part, as well.

The guests were seated on rows of white chairs
A sound system was rigged up in the trees tha
provided shade and Beethoven's 'Song of Joy' sig
nalled the start of the wedding procession. The
children set off down the aisle, John dictating the
action—'One, two, three, throw'—and the others
copied his hurling a handful of rose-petals into the
air with perfect timing.

It made everyone smile, even Max and Hans and
Guy who'd flown in for the wedding. The three
men were bachelors and had been very curious
about the woman Fletcher wanted to share his life
with, having not found one themselves. She'd felt
them trying to analyse the relationship, and told
them straight out to stop using their brains and get
in touch with their instincts.

'I married her for her smart mouth,' Fletcher had
dryly remarked, his eyes twinkling pleasure in her
ability to pinpoint basic truths about life.

'And no doubt her beauty,' Hans had put in.

'Not to mention a very understanding heart,'
Guy had said with a wry twist.

Max had nodded to Fletcher. 'Look at him.
Tamalyn has the gift of making him happy.'

On which point they'd all agreed.

Lonely men, Tammy had thought, just as Fletcher

had been, and told them they'd be very welcome in her and Fletcher's home any time they came to Sydney.

She was glad they were here, glad that so many people had come to share this shining day with her and Fletcher. Friendship, love, caring and sharing… it was what everyone wanted in their lives, what everyone needed, and she had it all today. A song of joy was beating through her as she finally set out down the aisle, walking towards the man who'd made everything right for her.

He smiled his dazzling smile, but this time it radiated love for her, and she smiled her love right back at him.

They stood together, exchanging the marriage vows without the slightest shadow of doubt that they would be kept. The insecurity they had both felt with each other was completely gone. They were one and nothing would ever separate them again, not in their minds and hearts.

The wedding celebrant declared them husband and wife.

They kissed.

As John rushed from his grandmother's side to join his mother and father, Celine remarked in a tone of immense satisfaction. 'Well that's it, gang! Six weddings!'

'And a baby,' Fletcher said, scooping John up to

be cuddled, his eyes twinkling his pleasure in bot
his bride and his son.

A baby who hadn't been planned, Tammy though
but a child who would always know he was loved.

That was more than good enough.

It was life at its best.

* * * * *

Turn the page for an exclusive extract from
THE PRINCE'S CAPTIVE WIFE
by
Marion Lennox

Bedded and wedded—by blackmail!

Nine years ago Prince Andreas Karedes left
Australia to inherit his royal duties, but unbe-
knownst to him he left a woman pregnant.

Innocent young Holly tragically lost their
baby and remained on her parents' farm to be
near her tiny son's final resting place, wishing Andreas would return!

A royal scandal is about to break: a dirt-dig-
ging journalist has discovered Holly's secret,
so Andreas forces his childhood sweetheart to
come and face him! Passion runs high as Andreas issues an ultimatum: to avoid scandal,
Holly must become his royal bride!

"SHE WAS ONLY SEVENTEEN?"

"We're talking ten years ago. I was barely out of my teens myself."

"Does that make a difference?" The uncrowned king of Aristo stared across his massive desk at his younger brother, his aquiline face dark with fury. "Have we not had enough scandal?"

"Not of my making." Prince Andreas Christos Karedes, third in line to the Crown of Aristo, stood his ground against his older brother with the disdain he always used in this family of testosterone-driven males. His father and brothers might be acknowledged womanizers, but Andreas made sure his affairs were discreet.

"Until now," Sebastian said. "Not counting your singularly spectacular divorce, which had a massive impact. But this is worse. You will have to sort it before it explodes over all of us."

"How the hell can I sort it?"

"Get rid of her."

"You're not saying…"

"Kill her?" Sebastian smiled up at his younge brother, obviously rejecting the idea—though tinge of regret in his voice said the option wasn altogether unattractive.

And Andreas even sympathized. Since the father's death, all three brothers had been dragge through the mire of the media spotlight, and the po litical unrest was threatening to destroy them. I their thirties, impossibly handsome, wealthy beyon belief, indulged and feted, the brothers were nov facing realities they had no idea what to do with.

"Though if I was our father…" Sebastian added and Andreas shuddered. Who knew what the ol king would have done if he'd discovered Holly' secret? Thank God he'd never found out. Not tha King Aegeus could have taken the moral hig ground. It was, after all, his father's past action that had gotten them into this mess.

"You'll make a better king than our father eve was," Andreas said softly. "What filthy dealin made him dispose of the royal diamond?"

"That's my concern," Sebastian said. Ther could be no royal coronation until the diamon was found—they all knew that—but the way th media was baying for blood there might not be coronation even then. Without the diamond th

ules had changed. If any more scandals broke…
"This girl…"

"Holly."

"You remember her?"

"Of course I remember her."

"Then she'll be easy to find. We'll buy her off—
do whatever it takes, but she mustn't talk to anyone."

"If she wanted to make a scandal she could have
done it years ago."

"So it's been simmering in the wings for years.
To have it surface now…" Sebastian rose and fixed
Andreas with a look that was almost as deadly as
the one used by the old king. "It can't happen,
brother. We have to make sure she's not in a
position to bring us down."

"I'll contact her."

"You'll go nowhere near her until we're sure of
her reaction. Not even a phone call, brother. For all
we know her phones are already tapped. I'll have
her brought here."

"I can arrange…"

"You stay right out of it until she's on our soil.
You're heading the corruption inquiry. With Alex
on his honeymoon with Maria—of all the times for
him to demand to marry, this must surely be the
worst—I need you more than ever. If you leave
now and this leaks, we can almost guarantee losing
the crown."

"So how do you propose to persuade her to come?"

"Oh, I'll persuade her," Sebastian said grimly. "She's only a slip of a girl. She might be your past but there's no way she's messing with our future."

* * * * *

Be sure to look for
THE PRINCE'S CAPTIVE WIFE
by Marion Lennox,
available September 2009
from Harlequin Presents®!